MURDER BY
Health Proxy

Based on a True Story

DAWN LISS

PAGE PUBLISHING, INC.
New York, NY

First originally published by Page Publishing, Inc. 2018

ISBN 978-1-64214-971-5 (Paperback)
ISBN 978-1-64350-564-0 (Hardcover)
ISBN 978-1-64214-972-2 (Digital)

Printed in the United States of America

This book is dedicated to my most admired writer, the late Thomas Sewell, coauthor of the Moe Berg book published in 1974 by Little, Brown and Co. Tom was and has been one of the most influential men in my life. He always encouraged me to write a book and was my biggest supporter in everything I did. Tom made me realize that no one ever dies unless you let them. Their spirit is always with you and is better than any friend. It is an unconditional feeling that lives inside of you and, if nurtured properly, can bring out the best in you and others. He was the editor of our magazine *The Furry Friends* (a free animal magazine that was distributed throughout New England). Tom believed in me. Tom made me smile when I was sad. He lifted me when I was down, and he always told me I could do anything and always encouraged me to write a novel! He believed in me like no one else in my life ever believed in me. His heart was made of pure gold, and his love for me was sincere and pure. He always said, "Dawnie, you're the tops. You can do anything you set your mind to, and you should write a book." As I sit here at my computer writing, I feel Tom with his hand on my shoulder telling me what an incredible story I am writing! He will forever live in my heart, and his inspiration has lived and will live inside of me until eternity. Thank you, my friend. I love you always, and I know you are helping me as I write this book. You are the best!

Love you always,
Dawn

When I despair, I remember that all through history the way of truth and love have always won. There have been tyrants and murderers, and for a time, they can seem invincible, but in the end, they always fall. Think of it—always.

—Mahatma Gandhi

Foreword

In today's society, we have an epidemic of white-collar murder. Elderly people especially are being murdered by their caretakers and the people that supposedly love them. Let us ask ourselves the question: How about when there is a whole bunch of money thrown into the scene?

After experiencing the death of my best friend, at the hands of his health proxy, it was a disgrace that his obituary read she was his long-time companion. She was his murderess. This type of crime goes unnoticed every day, especially when someone of stature or someone that is believed to have their own money commits this unimaginable crime. Why is it so hard for us to believe that a person would murder someone we love for money? Humanity has such an aversion to death as we know it. The reason is most likely that decent human beings do not murder people they love; only psychopaths and murderers can display this behavior with no remorse. How often does this crime "murder by health proxy" happen? How often does the health proxy get put behind bars for murder?

Today in America and I am sure throughout the world, this has become a white-collar crime that seems acceptable when there is no one to follow through on any investigation. Perhaps this is the reason why our television shows about wives that murder husbands and just the opposite or people murdering people that are close to them go unaccountable until they are made into entertainment. The crime of murder by health proxy seems almost acceptable in our society because most people do not have the depth or intuition that it takes to flush out a killer. What is the difference between a person getting shot dead on the streets of Chicago and the person that died in a small town with the help of their health proxy? Whether it be denying him of the medical needs to sustain life, which was the case here, or pulling the trigger of an AK-47, murder is murder. Now, let's throw a big bunch of money into the mix!

White-collar murder is on the rise in America, folks! The more we allow it to go unnoticed, the more murders will take place by individuals that have both the power and especially the money. It could be a little money or a lot of money. The fact is that this happens every day, and the culprit is usually the person complaining about how much they had done for the deceased.

Love and death have no boundaries, so when you truly love someone, it never occurs to you how difficult it was for you when they are the one that is going to die.

My deceased Jesuit professor, Dr. Thomas, would always say, "We never learn anything about life until we have a good emotional shake up! We are trembling to the very core of our existence and react with tears of joy or sorrow." Experiencing something that has never happened to us before is part of learning the lessons life has to teach.

When someone dies, when someone is born, and when there is a divorce or a suicide or overdose, we all rethink our lives and wonder why.

As told to me by my professor, there are only questions. The answers are there for the taking, but how many of us are willing to go the distance or do the work it takes investigators sometimes twenty years to solve? Most of the television shows we watch about incredible murder mysteries are not solved or made into TV shows until ten or twenty years after the crime is committed, some even longer. This book is intended to spark the curiosity in everyone's mind as we all know someone that is now deceased and we all have questions as to the why and how it happened.

I suppose I am writing this book as an investigatory lesson into my own thoughts and beliefs of my own experience about an unnecessary death of someone that will live in my heart forever.

I Need to Tell You a Story

I lived in the small coastal town of Eastport, Connecticut. Recently, a murder took place that resulted in the death of a man that I had lived with and loved. He was the town veterinarian for over twenty-eight years. Facts were brought to the police before his death. An elder abuse report could not get filed by another local prominent doctor that had just left the rehab facility in which he witnessed the abuse and lack of medical care. The deceased, Dr. Sahib Koury, had his health proxy sitting by his bedside.

Linda Muldrew, a stout woman with nicotine-stained teeth, owned the local Eastport apothecary. A woman who had access to any drug made, her first and only husband died in the apothecary some forty years before at the age of forty-three from a massive heart attack. That seems a bit young for a massive heart attack. A pharmacist, Bill Muldrew, who had built and insured the pharmacy leaving it to his wife Linda . . . and so the story begins.

When I moved to Eastport in 1989, I was given a very good recommendation from the previous veterinarian I had worked for. I interviewed on a Wednesday with Dr. Koury, owner and founder of Eastport Animal Hospital, the first animal hospital located in the town since its inception.

He was a very tall attractive man with crooked teeth. He spoke with a very heavy Arabic accent and was a very devout Muslim. I remember seeing a small woven prayer rug in his office that I suspected was for afternoon prayers to Allah. He was very forward with me and asked why I wanted to work there. I explained to him that I had recently left Troy and was now living just a few miles up the road and needed a job. I could tell from his demeanor that he knew my moving was for other reasons, which it was. I had recently broken off a ten-year relationship with a married man. He knew from the doctor that I had previously worked for that my former boyfriend was much older than I and involved in organized crime. I knew nothing of his dealings, but I did know that he always had thousands of dollars in his pocket and seemed to have a lot of power among his friends. I moved to Eastport to break free of his illegal activities that I knew would one day hurt me.

Dr. Koury was not at all enthusiastic about me working there, but I thought for sure I would get the job because I was a very good employee, and I certainly loved animals. I left his office hoping he would call me but not knowing if he ever would. That was that!

During the next few weeks, my life was filled with tumultuous arguments and disagreements with my ex and he would come and go to my new residence as he pleased. I had four beautiful dogs that I was allowed to keep at the house. I had rented right on the river. My dogs were my sanity! My lifestyle after ten years had become so dependent on Mr. Ex that I needed to work badly as I did not want anything from him anymore and the house I was renting was quite costly.

One Saturday morning, about three weeks after my interview with the good doctor, I was very hung over. I had been quite upset over my current situation at twenty-six years old—not married, no children, and a married man that would not let go. It was around eleven in the morning when the phone started ringing and my head started pounding with a banging headache. I waited for several rings before I could compose myself and answer. Apparently, my voice was quite telling as I answered because there was a sudden angered voice on the other end that said, "Is this the time you are going to wake up when you come to work for me?" I immediately recognized the heavy Arabic accent and knew it was the doc! I jumped up out of bed and replied, "No, Dr. Koury. I would always be there on time. I have had some personal problems this weekend, and I am not feeling very well.

With that, he said, "Be here Monday morning at seven." Then, he hung up.

I was so elated! I jumped out of bed and ran to the shower. The rest of the day was very productive, and I was trying to decide how I would do my hair and what I would wear to look perfect on Monday. I was already scared to death of him!

Thank God the rest of my weekend was quiet, and I had some time to recuperate. Mr. Ex did not show up, which was fine by me. I knew he was involved with an Argentinian girl. He was dealing cocaine with her, and I wanted no part of him or her in my life anymore.

Monday morning came; and I jumped out of bed, showered, and dressed and was on my way by six thirty. The animal hospital was only five minutes away, so I waited about fifteen minutes until Heather arrived. She was a beautiful girl with blue eyes and gorgeous flowing natural blond hair. She had told me she was married, but I thought surely that Dr. Koury had to be in love with her and they had a relationship. Heather was gorgeous! Every man fell in love with her at first glance! That observation could not have been further from the truth. Heather was the most upstanding lady I had ever met in my life. She explained to me briefly before the doctor arrived to stay quiet as he did not like noise and did not like anyone talking too much, not even to clients! (Boy, was I in trouble?) I was definitely a talker, especially to the animals! He arrived about an hour later. He came in and went straight to his office and never said a word. He performed surgeries in the early mornings on Monday, Wednesday, and Fridays.

This happened back in 1989. I was so happy to be there, so I followed the rules for the first few days; and every time I would try to talk about something, he would tell me to be quiet! There was a quality of dignity about him that I had never seen in any other man. He was an old-school Egyptian and very dominant and was very good to his clients. He would still charge the older women $20 for their office visits, no matter what he did. He was a kind Saint Francis–like man with a heart of gold that touched all of his clients deeply. People loved him, especially the women.

I had always been attracted to older men as my dad was a weekend warrior with alcohol and could be very violent at times. I always sought out the affections of older men, but the Doc was one tough cookie! My ex was thirty years my senior, and it never bothered me. I always felt safe and protected. As a younger girl, I was always looking for the approval of an older man because nothing I ever did was right with my dad. Please understand that I am not trying to demonize my father. He made me the strong, confident, hardworking woman I am today. The doc knew my ex was much older than I and certainly older than him. He had learned all about my ex from the previous vet I had worked for. I did not know at the time, but the Doc was told that my ex was a very dangerous man and he had better not interfere with my life; otherwise, there would be consequences. This was not far from the truth, as my ex still tried to claim ownership rights on me even though he was married and had other girlfriends. It took ten years, but I finally came to realize that my beauty and loyalty were just not enough.

After working there a week, I was so mesmerized by the Doc. My life had new meaning. I adored Heather in the office. She was so kind and caring. She had been working for the doc since he had opened some twenty years. Heather was loyal, quiet, and beautiful . . . everything the Doc loved in a woman, and I know he loved her. She in turn loved him but in a fatherly way. Heather was in no way attracted to him physically as I learned a few months later.

I worked as hard and as best I knew every day for him. I was kind to the animals, and he knew I had four dogs, which he thought was too many! I knew in my heart that everything he knew about me he associated it with my ex whom he came to like in a very strange manner. I am sure now that he treated him so kindly because of me. He knew my ex drove a Mercedes, and he saw the diamonds on my fingers, and I am sure he thought I was the most materialistic woman he had ever met and money was my God! This could not have been further from the truth. I came from a very humble background, a fifty-acre chicken farm in Burlington, Vermont, where I spent my high school years with my mother, father, and brother as my two older sisters were married by then with children. Due to my second oldest sister's pregnancy, my dad decided that he would move "me" into the woods so I would not get pregnant at sixteen as my sister (his pet) did. I spent my high school years with 38,000 chickens coming in and out of the barn every seven weeks and working in that barn from five in the morning until I went to school. He would wait for me when the bus dropped me off at three; and I would run into the house, change into my barn clothes, and go into the barn to "cull chickens." Culling means killing the sick so the healthy would grow! We had 38,000 every seven weeks. When we first moved there, I had refused to cull chickens; but if you knew my father, you do not say you were not going to do what he told you to do. You do it, or there were consequences. He was a very stern handsome man that was a bit frustrated about not becoming a wealthy businessman like some of his friends. He managed to take most of that frustration and anger out on me on a daily basis. My nickname was "Marria." To this day, I think he started calling me that because when we still lived in Troy. I landed a part at the local high school as one of the children in *The Sound of Music*. I was only in eighth grade, and I tried out for the part against all the other kids in the schools of the city. I was never congratulated for it, but it got me out of the house a few nights a week away from his usual reign of terror! I was "Louisa" in *The Sound of Music*, one of the children. I sang "I flit, I float. I fleetly flee, I fly. Good night. Good night. Goodbye!"

CHAPTER 2

My New Job

As the weeks rolled by, I became more helplessly in love with this unusual man, the Doc. He constantly told me to be quiet and to stop talking so much. I would always answer him back in a loving way. After a few weeks, I felt something that I had never felt deep down inside. I was beginning to feel that he cared about me and maybe even liked me as a woman. I tried to obey him and his demands at work. I am a bit of a rebellion, and I believe in my heart he was up for a challenge! I wasn't just another pretty face. All the girls that worked at the hospital were attractive. He always surrounded himself with pretty woman. There were only four of us, but my hours were the longest of anyone else's on a weekly basis. I was the only one willing to work every Saturday or anytime because I truly loved the animals. I felt like the hospital was a part of me. I had found a new home.

It was a very small animal hospital located underneath a local plaza that was hidden in the back. There were no big signs posted or any advertisement. The hospital was full of loyal clients that Dr. Koury had established over his twenty-eight years of providing love, care, and psychotherapy to all those who visited him. He would actually yell at the dogs from the small office beside the front desk! With his thick Arabic accent, he would say things to the dog (with the owner standing right there). "Don't you think I know you by now?" he would ask the dog. "Don't start your bullshit with me. You act like jerk, I treat you like jerk," he would say in his clear-throated

Arabic accent! I would laugh so hard, and it was difficult to keep a straight face when the client came out. People loved him. He would talk to the animals as if they were his children! He remembered every dog, cat, owner, and personalized every visit with his own signature style of love, compassion, discipline, and effectiveness! Whenever he would exclaim, "Don't you think I know you?" I assumed the dog gave him a very hard time on his previous yearly visit, which turned out to be the case. The Doc always made me feel more confident in my own abilities to work with animals. Whenever a large shepherd or rottweiler would pose a threat, he would call me in the small little patient room and tell me, "Hold the dog." I would quickly wrap its leash around his/her mouth and hold the dog with my entire body against the wall. He would give the dog/cat its shots, and all was good.

He was definitely a cat man and loved working more with cats than dogs. Dogs had too much personality . . . like me! He never complimented me on doing a good job or how I handled animals, but he continued to give me more hours.

Sometimes, on a Friday night, we would be at the hospital until nine or ten sewing up a dog that had been hit by a car. He would always mock me by saying things like "Are you stupid?" This was his way of showing affection as crazy as it may sound. I heard him many, many times speak to Heather in this manner. Every day, he would say things that today would be considered harassment, sexism, you name it. Heather and I would laugh! He would even put up one of his fingers, not the middle one, and say, "This is for you, Heather," when she would question his authority about anything! It was very funny, and his humor was dry and effective.

He worked from eight to twelve and went home from twelve to three and stayed open until six or whenever. People would call him at two in the morning, and he would meet them at the hospital and tend to their animal. His loyalty was paramount! You could *never* find a veterinarian like Dr. Koury today. He was loyal to a fault especially to his clients that had been loyal to him. He was an amazing man, selfless, committed to his practice, and kind to everyone.

In those days, the late eighties, we billed people if they did not have the money. Heather would do the billing every month, and I am sure he had thousands in outstanding services. He never hired an attorney to collect anything owed to him. He trusted that people would do the right thing, because he always did the right thing when it came to money. He never spent money on anything unless he needed it badly. His equipment was old, but it did the trick. If not, he would send his patient to one of his longtime veterinary friends for a second opinion. He would be sure to call them first and warn them about not charging them too much money. I would roll over laughing when he would talk to the veterinarian I had previously worked for. They had known each other since Dr. Koury's arrival in Eastport. He would call Dr. Sosa and say, "You bastard, I am sending someone there for an ultrasound. Don't you charge them too much!" Apparently, the two doctors had drunk together and worked together at the same animal hospital when Dr. Koury had just come here from NYC.

He started out loading trucks on the docks in New York. Then, he became a taxi driver while he studied English so he could take the veterinary exam in the United States and get his license. He passed his first time. He attended veterinary school in Egypt. He was shy, intelligent, hardworking, and very, very careful with money. Our medical dispensary had only the amount of prescription drugs that he knew he would need for the month. He never ordered anything that would be wasted. He did every dogs stool sample himself under a small microscope in the tiny lab we had. Eventually, he taught me all the different parasites to look for and what they looked like. Basically, we had to define the type of worms the dog or cat had in order to treat it properly. Some of his methods were very old fashioned, but they worked.

After two months of doing my best and trying to figure out what made the Doc tick, I still had no clue. He would sometimes spend hours in his office reading veterinary journals and textbooks. Sometimes, he would call Egypt and talk to his family, and I would hear the beautiful Arabic dialect he would speak from behind the door of his tiny office. Once he was finished, he would walk out, continue working, and never say a word.

I would always wonder if he was thinking about me as I constantly thought about him or if he liked me or anything! There were no answers with him. He was a complete mystery of a man. He showed no emotion about anything, and I was the exact opposite.

I always wore my heart on my sleeve, and I was still dealing with Mr. Ex. Mr. Ex knew I had changed because I never called him or contacted him. He still continued to come to the house, and I would still go out to eat dinner with him when he was in his right mind. Old habits do die hard! I did love him, but I was so preoccupied with my newfound love, Dr. Koury, that anything Mr. Ex did was fine by me! I was struggling financially, and Mr. Ex would always leave money for me as he did for ten years. I did not hate him. I hated what he had become. He was running with some real bad people in the cocaine trade, particularly a woman that had just allowed her innocent boyfriend to do ten years in the federal penitentiary. He was in the car with her cousin when they stopped him. Two kilos of cocaine were in the trunk of her cousin's car. Billy (her then baby father) had no idea they were even there! He was being used as a fool! He did ten years for that mistake, while Mr. Ex began grooming her during our soon-to-be permanent separation.

The Doc saved my life! I mean that wholeheartedly! I probably would be dead if it was not for him. I guess I am writing this book because I was not allowed to save him from his murderess! He saved me from a life that would have led me down the road of destruction and my demise. It is no wonder I was so drawn to him. He truly was my savior!

One Sunday night, Mr. Ex arrived at the house as high as a kite! He took all my jewelry off the counter and put it in his pocket.

I said, "What the hell are you doing?"

He said he knew I was screwing the doctor and that I was having an affair with him. This was not true at that time, so I became very enraged. I lunged at him and grabbed his shirt and screamed to the top of my lungs!

"You are high as a kite, and you are screwing Liliana, the Argentinian girl. You will end up in jail just like Billy."

This went on all night until my neighbor that was quite a distance away came over and asked me if I wanted him to call the police. I ran out and begged him not to. Once the neighbor came, Mr. Ex put down my jewelry (as he knew I had his father's gold Rolex), which I threatened I would never give to him. It was about five in the morning when Mr. Ex finally left. I had to be at work in two hours! I was a mess!

I jumped in the shower and tried to get myself together, but I was shaken to the core. We had never in all of the ten years been physical with each other. He never lifted his hands to me. He just kept pushing me away, not to mention the fact that he also always had a piece on his belt! I was a brave little girl, with a lot of chutzpah!

My eyes were red from not sleeping, and my head was spinning. I knew Dr. Koury would see that there was something wrong with me. I feared that I would be fired because I looked like I was on drugs!

We started surgery right away, and I was dead silent. He was always quiet, but on that day, you could have heard a pin drop in the small surgery room. Then, came the big question.

"What's wrong with you? You are too quiet."

I said, "I just didn't sleep well."

He responded, "You must think I am stupid or something?"

With that remark, tears started flowing down my cheeks at a very rapid rate. I could hardly hold the surgery instruments in place, but I stayed strong and tried to act as if I could deal with my problem.

He told me to clean my eyes, and he wanted to talk to me in the office after appointments. He did not say it mean. He said it in a very gentle and caring manner. After surgery was over, I couldn't stop crying, so I retreated to the tiny break room and told Heather. I had confided in her about my situation many times. She had met Mr. Ex several times and liked him as everyone did. He was good to everyone, and only I knew his darkest secrets. We continued working as if nothing happened, and Heather went home a little before three. The

Doc came back fifteen minutes before three, and it was just he and I for the rest of the afternoon until six. He got back from lunch a little earlier that day. He called me into his office and told me to sit down.

"What's wrong?" he said in a very caring way.

I immediately started crying quietly and told him that Mr. Ex was dealing with very bad people and I was afraid for my life. I also stated that Mr. Ex came and went to my house anytime he wanted to, and I did not want him there. I did not know what to do anymore. He told me to stay calm and everything will work out. I had no idea what he was talking about. By the time six in the evening came, guess who walked in the front door of the animal hospital? Larger than life, Mr. Ex. Dr. Koury greeted him with a very warm hello and told him to come into his office! I was in shock!

"How are you?" the Doc exclaimed. "Sit down," he said.

He and Mr. Ex were in his office with the door open talking like they had known each other for years! They had never met! Suddenly, I felt a sense of security that I had never felt in my life. It wasn't like any other feeling I had ever experienced. A warm glow encompassed my body that made me feel very safe. I asked myself, "What the hell is going on here? What is happening? Why is he befriending the man I told him hurts me so much?" A million questions rolled through my head that seemed like a runaway train.

Mr. Ex started exiting the Doc's office and looked over at me kindly and said, "I will see you at the house." My heart sank to my feet again as I could feel danger lurking in the shadows of his presence in my home. He walked out of the office and shut the door. I was totally bewildered and did not say a word. I was trying my best to comprehend what had just happened. Where the hell am I? What is going on?

The Doc could see I was unhinged knowing that Mr. Ex was headed back to the house. He called me into his office once again and told me to sit down. He wrote his home phone number on a piece of paper and told me to call him right away if Mr. Ex starts his nonsense. He promised he would come and take me out of there immediately.

Who is this man? I kept asking myself on that long drive home. He is going to protect me or save me from this nothingness of a life I have lived with Mr. Ex? I did not want him to get hurt, and I knew Mr. Ex would do anything to anyone that he thought might impede his ownership rights to his ten-year possession. *Me!*

The Doc's concern for me made me feel very strong and confident. I was not afraid anymore. I would confront Mr. Ex head on but with a civil tongue. I may even try the Doc's method, being quiet.

I got to the house, but his car was not there. Little did I know he was inside the house. I let the dogs out of their kennel and hugged them all and stayed outside for a minute. I saw him through the big glass windows that faced the Eastport river. I was about to confront my worst nightmare. I did not want him going to the animal hospital! I did not want him to know the Doc! I did not want him to come and go as he pleased! I was sick of all of it! I was especially sick that he had gotten so close to my most guarded secret—my love for the Doc.

I walked in the house with a confident air and said, "Where is your car?"

He said, "Give me the keys. You are driving my Mercedes, aren't you?"

"I didn't quite understand."

He then said, "If you don't have a car, then you can't work for your boyfriend!"

He grabbed the keys out of my hand and ran out the door! I now had no transportation. Actually, I was glad he left that quickly. I could walk to work if I had to, and I knew Heather would give me a ride. I really didn't care. However, it was an excuse for me to call the Doc because I knew he was genuinely concerned about my well-being after he had heard Mr. Ex say he was going to the house, also after I had told the Doc that afternoon about his involvement with drugs and very bad people.

I dialed his number and said, "I just want you to know that I am okay."

He responded, "Where is he?"

I told him what had happened, and he told me to call Heather for morning pickups and that he would take me home in the afternoons for the three-hour lunch break. He would also pick me back up to bring me back to work until six and drive me home to make sure I was safe. He told me to lock the doors and windows and if anything happened that night to call him.

I thought I had died and went to heaven! He liked me! He cared about me! But most of all, he wanted to protect me! Honestly speaking, I did need protection because Mr. Ex was known for his escapades. He never did it himself. He would have one of his hoods carry out his misdeeds. All who knew him feared him, but not the Doc!

CHAPTER 3

My Romance

I sit here and think of the Carly Simon song: "My romance doesn't have to have a moon beam. My romance doesn't mean that much to me." My romance with the Doc was the most love I had ever felt from a man in my life. I am now fifty-six years of age, I was twenty-five when my romance with the Doc occurred.

All was quiet on the home front, and I would get calls from Mr. Ex, but he had no apparent reason to come to the house. I told him to stay away from me and go to his newfound drug-dealing girlfriend! He was quite pissed, but I really did not care at all. My concern was only for my safety and the Doc's safety. About a week after things calmed down, my mom had offered her small Honda car to me. She had been sick and was not working anymore. She never complained. The truth of her illness would not be told to me until several years later when she was dying.

I went to see my mother every day to check on her and also tell her about my newfound love. She thought it was great! What mother does not want their daughter to marry a doctor? I would tell her how funny he talked and how mysterious he was and that he was Egyptian. She loved the saga! She had liked Mr. Ex very much but now hated him because she feared for my life and safety as well. She encouraged my relationship with the Doc every day and told me, "Honey, with a man like this, you have to go very slow." I knew she was right. She was always right. She was my mother. She loved me more than any human being on this earth could ever love me. I needed her more than anyone in this world. She would always give me good advice, especially when it came to men. I listened to her every word. "Take it slow," she would say, "just take it slow."

The Doc knew my mom was sick, but he too did not know she had a life-threatening illness. She had told me to make him a nice dinner and offer to bring it to his house so that "just in case" Mr. Ex would know nothing.

I took her advice. I went to work the next day; and during morning surgery, when we were alone, I asked him if he liked roasted chicken with potatoes and carrots. With his very dry humor, he gave a slight smile and said, "You know how to cook?" I explained to him that I was a very good cook. I told him the story of how my mother would sit me on the counter when I was a very young girl. She prepared our meals and would tell me everything she was doing. Apparently, I convinced him because we set a date for the next night. It was a Saturday, and we only had a half day. We closed at one every Saturday. I would have time to cook the meal to bring to his home. I did not even know where he lived! I had to ask him the next day.

In my heart of hearts, I had to tell Heather what was happening here. I needed her approval. She had been with the Doc for some twenty-eight years, and I did not want her to resent or hate me for pursuing a relationship with him. I needed her permission. I respected her so much as a friend and a woman.

After doc left that afternoon, I asked Heather if I could talk to her at the local restaurant and bar, Ishmael's, that evening around seven. She agreed to meet me there. What was I going to say to her? I didn't want her to hate me. I didn't want her to think that my intentions were not sincere. I realized that the truth would be the best way to explain myself as Heather was a master at the truth. She was as honest and sincere as they came, a true friend. In the short time we had worked together, we had gone out for cocktails and told our war stories about the men in our lives, and I trusted her with my every breath. I truly love Heather to this day. She was my only friend.

I arrived that night at Ishmael's, and Heather was already there. I had worked, so I had to change and shower. When I walked in, she acted normal because she did not know what I was about to tell her or how I felt about the Doc. I placed my hand on her arm and said, "Heather, I need to talk to you." With that, I proceeded to tell her how I had become so fond of the Doc and that I was going to make him dinner the next day and bring it to his house.

She was a bit shocked and said, "What do you find attractive about him?"

I said, "I didn't really know, but I really liked being around him."

She laughed because Heather had no physical attraction to the Doc in twenty-eight years! She was married with two beautiful children and what seemed to be a perfect marriage. She told me to do whatever made me happy and that she did not care. She also warned me that he was a tough cookie, which I already knew. I was so happy Heather knew. I had her approval, and I was good to go!

Saturday, I opened the animal hospital by quarter to seven. I did the menial tasks around the office that we did every day. I was so happy about my first date with the Doc!

He was so calm and laid back all the time. Nothing ruffled his feathers. I was a ticking time bomb waiting to explode. I maintained my composure throughout the half day and did not say much. I was playing it safe because I wanted this moment so badly. My heart was pounding with happiness, one beat at a time.

He always left before I did, and as he was walking out the door, I said, "I will be there with dinner around seven." He looked at me and said, "Okay." That was it. I was so happy!

I ran to the market and bought the best of everything. I rushed home and prepared my chicken and placed it in the oven so it would be hot and ready when I was leaving. I took my shower, fixed my hair, and wore beautiful clothes. I also took off most of my jewelry and hid it in the house. I knew he hated the diamond rings I wore from Mr. Ex. He thought I was very materialistic but did not know that they were a possession I had never asked for. Mr. Ex loved jewelry and would give it to me all the time. Only God knows where it came from! I don't want to know.

Within a few hours, I was ready. I felt like I was going on my first date! It was so special. He was such a private man. No one went to his house.

I called Heather and told her I was going, and she told me to have a good time. She had known that I had been having an awful time with Mr. Ex, so I think she was happy that I was happy.

I drove to the other side of Eastport, and as luck would have it, it came to me. I had landed in a hot air balloon in his backyard a year before! Talk about the laws of attraction! When I ever drove down the lane where he lived, I knew that I belonged there. The hot air balloon landing? It all seemed so surreal. I definitely knew what to start the conversation with for an opener! He came to the door and helped me with the food. I told him that I could not believe he lived there. He said that the hot air balloons land in the fields near his house sometimes. I was in heaven. On the way to his house, I remembered listening to a two-song cassette disc that I would play over and over again by Debbie Gibson: "I get lost in your eyes when I feel . . . da da da da. You can take me to the sky . . . it's like being lost in heaven, when I'm lost in your eyes."

I love to sing and have always associated songs with relationships. I am sure I wore that cassette out! We had a wonderful dinner, and he was so loving and caring. We held each other for hours. I could not let go of him. He took my hand and we went into the bedroom, and we made love and I was in heaven. I never wanted to leave, but I had to take care of my dogs. I got home about two in the morning and called him as he requested so he knew I arrived safely. I knew this was the beginning of the most love I had ever experienced from any man. I never wanted it to end.

CHAPTER 4

The End of Mr. Ex

Two weeks had passed, and I continued to get the usual harassment call from Mr. Ex.

"How is your new boyfriend?" he would ask.

I would ignore his question and ask what he was calling for. On that particular day, he said, "Well, since you don't have a new boyfriend, I am coming over later to see you and pick up some of my clothing. Maybe we will go out to dinner?"

"No," I replied. "I do not want to go to dinner, and please be there after six to get your clothes as I am going to my mom's."

I was not going to my mom's. I would visit her on my three-hour lunch breaks, and I would go over to doc's house at night with dinner and come home about ten or eleven. Mr. Ex was definitely interfering with my plans.

I told the Doc that he had called and he was coming to the house. I could see by the expression on his face. He was concerned for me and did not like the fact that Mr. Ex was coming to my house. I assured him that I would be all right. As soon as he left, I would go straight to his house. He said, "I will wait for you to call me after he leaves before you come over." I was afraid that Mr. Ex would follow me to see where I was going, so I anticipated making this a short visit! I had all his things packed neatly in a suitcase so he could pick it up and be on his way.

I waited at the house until I saw the blue Mercedes pull in. He came to the door with a big smile and a few bags of Chinese food, all my favorites. I asked him why he was bringing all this food. He stated that he wanted to sit and talk to me. I am thinking to myself how badly I wanted to get out of there to go and see the Doc. I also knew that if the Doc did not hear from me within the hour, he would be worried. I tried to play it very cool by saying that my mom was waiting for me. He said, "Why don't you take her some Chinese food?" I told him that was a good idea. He then grabbed my hand and said he needed to talk to me. He told me how much he loved me and he did not want our relationship to end because he had missed me so much in the past two weeks.

Oh dear God, help me. I explained to him that he was still married and I am quite sure he is still with Liliana and our ten-year relationship has come to an end. He became very angry and accused me of being the one that had a boyfriend, and we went back and forth until I finally said, "I do not want to do this! It does not matter! It is over! I will always love you, but I do not want a life with you." With that, he said he did not believe me!

I managed to get myself ready to leave and wrapped up the Chinese food to bring to my mom (so he thought). It had been almost two hours, and I knew the Doc had to be worried. Mr. Ex was furious with me and said he would stay at the house and wait for me to get back. He did have a key, so there was not much I could do but leave. There were no cell phones in those days, so I could not call the Doc while I was on my way to his house. I drove very fast and drove down the long dark lane where he lived. I knew he was going to be upset, but he never showed his emotions. He was standing at the door because he saw my headlights coming down the driveway. He knew I was very nervous and upset. I got out of the car and tried to make light of my previous confrontation by saying, "Do you want some Chinese food?"

He said, "Where did you get that from?"

I proceeded to tell him that Mr. Ex was lying in wait for me back at the house, and I knew he did not want me to go back there. He also knew that I had to confront my demons from the past, and I had a responsibility with my dogs. I stayed with him for just a few hours, hoping that Mr. Ex would get tired of waiting and leave.

Unfortunately, he did not. The Doc had given me instructions to call him when I got home as if I was calling my mom to let her know I made it home okay. Then, he would ask the questions and I would answer.

I arrived at the house and the Mercedes was still in the driveway, and he was asleep on the couch. "Good God," I thought to myself. He thinks he is spending the night. My head started racing, and I just wanted him to leave. I did not want to fight. I just wanted him to go. I did not want to answer any more questions from him either. He then said he would spend the night on the couch because he was too tired to drive back to the city. My heart sunk into my chest. My bedroom was upstairs, and there was a telephone beside the bed, so I knew I could call the Doc and lock the bedroom door. I took a blanket and two pillows off the downstairs bed and gave it to Mr. Ex. I expressed to him that I was no longer comfortable with him staying over, but I would make an exception tonight. I wanted to leave early in the morning as I had to be in work at seven. He was very pissed and continued to try to speak to me about the ten years we had together and all the good times and there would be more. I did not want any more, but I did not want a war that night either. I stayed quiet and went up to my bedroom and locked the door after saying good night. I told him I was going to call my mom to let her know I was home. I know he did not believe me, but I really did not care. I changed into pajamas and locked the bedroom door and also put a chair under the doorknob. I dialed up the Doc and spoke very quietly. "I am home, and he is downstairs on the couch. He is staying here and I do not want him here, and I don't know what to do about this anymore."

The Doc could tell I was crying because I missed and loved him and did not want to be near or in the same house as my once ten-year companion. He said, "I am going to take care of it."

I said, "What do you mean?"

He said nothing. He then told me to call him if there were any problems and to get to the hospital early so I could get out of there. The next day was Saturday. I knew Mr. Ex would leave early to be at his factory. I deliberately stayed in my bedroom upstairs until he left at five in the morning. I am sure he was eager to contact his new girlfriend, the Argentinian drug queen. She had a very strong hold on him. I had recognized his behavior many months before I had moved to Eastport. He was a totally different person.

I was so glad he was gone. As I was getting dressed for work, I kept asking myself over and over again, "How am I going to get him out of my life completely?" I have to get out of this house too! Once again, I was confused and did not know where to run.

Today was Saturday, a half day at the hospital, so I would have time to visit my mom after work and then see the Doc that evening. We worked side by side that morning, and I knew he could tell that I was lost in my thoughts. I told him I was going to see my mom and I would be over later with some dinner for him. He asked me how long I would be at my moms, and I said about an hour. He also asked what time I would be back at my house, and I said after three. He walked out of the office and said that he would see me later.

I cleaned up the hospital and drove over to see my mom. She was always laying on the couch due to chronic pain in her lower abdomen that she had. I had brought her some fried shrimp and scallops from the restaurant above the animal hospital. I knew it was her favorite, and she would get mad at me because she knew I did not have a lot of money. She did not want me spending my money on food for her. I would always laugh and say, "Too bad. You are getting it anyway!" She had no appetite anymore, so I would always bring her food that I knew she loved, just so she would eat. She was so happy about my relationship with the Doc and was so mad when I told her about Mr. Ex coming and staying the night before.

"You have to get out of there," she said. "Come here and live with your father and I."

Good God, my father was as tuff as nails! His cigar would permeate the entire house. Every time I walked out of there, I smelled like a cigar store Indian! My poor mother, she hated his smoking. I explained to her that I would have to find homes for my dogs and that would break my heart, but if need be, I would do it. I knew so many people from the animal hospital. I would be sure to place them with people I knew. After she gobbled up her seafood, we had a good laugh and I drove back to the house to feed the dogs. Ten minutes later, the phone rang. It was Mr. Ex.

He said, "I need you to come to Ishmael's restaurant right now!"

I explained to him that I had just got back from my mom's and work and needed to take a shower and I was busy.

He insisted very sternly. "I need you here. There is something we have to talk about now!"

"Okay, okay," I said, "but I am only staying twenty minutes."

"That's fine," he said, "just get here."

I changed my clothes and jumped in the car. I did not even bother to call the Doc because I was going to end this nonsense once and for all. Driving to the restaurant, only ten minutes away, I was thinking that I would move out of that house. I could live with my mom and dad temporarily just to be safe. My mom needed me.

I got to the restaurant, parked the car, and walked inside. As I looked over to the tables by the ocean, I saw Mr. Ex sitting with the Doc!

"Holy cow! This cannot be good," I thought to myself. As I walked over to the table, Mr. Ex got up from his chair; and in a very nasty tone, he said, "Choose the side you are going to sit at because that is where you will stay." I immediately sat down next to the Doc. We had lunch, and the Doc spoke very nicely and told Mr. Ex that I would be coming to live with him. He also told him that he is welcome at his home anytime and he would like to remain friends with him. As we were all leaving, Mr. Ex said to the Doc, "Why don't you show me where you live?"

"Sure," the Doc said.

I was behind Mr. Ex with my hands telling the Doc, "No!"

We all followed the Doc to his home, and Mr. Ex only stayed about ten minutes. I thought surely Mr. Ex was planning something bad for the Doc and my future. We never saw him again.

CHAPTER 5

My New Home

During the next week, I packed up my clothing and started looking for homes for my dogs. There was Murphy, a golden retriever; Mika, a chow; Moppy, an old English sheepdog; and Max, a huge puppy rottweiler, my four boys and guardians. I was so sad. The Doc had a big yard, but he had already told me that I could not have the dogs there because of his ten-year-old cat Nikita that was his other girlfriend. Oh how he loved that cat. I do know my dogs would have eaten her! I wanted to keep Murphy. He was my first dog ever and a golden retriever, and he would not hurt the cat. I pleaded with the Doc to let me keep Murphy. He finally suggested that I give Murphy to his next door neighbor that had two little girls. He said that I would see him every day. I was still so upset. I did manage to find wonderful homes for the other three. Max, the big rottweiler who was actually still a nine-month-old puppy, went to Heather's house, kennel, and all! I thanked her so much, and she loved him so much. I had previously worked in another local town as a bartender at the Old Country Lodge. The owner there loved my Old English sheepdog, Moppy. He was happy to take him for me, and his neighbor took the chow, Mika. Giving up Murphy was going to kill me. My dad would not let him stay at their house. I asked my new neighbor if he would take Murphy for his two little girls. I also told him we would take care of any medical needs. He agreed, and Murphy lived next door to me and the Doc. He waited for me every day. I was still heartbroken and resented the Doc very much because

I was not allowed to keep Murphy because of his cat. I knew Murphy would never hurt that cat.

About three weeks went by, and I noticed that the neighbor's wife was not coming home anymore and there was trouble amiss. Murphy would come to our door at ten in the evening because he had been left alone, and I would let him in. The Doc would get very stern with me and tell me, "No, you cannot have the dog in the house." I was so hurt by that. A few days later, it was thundering and lightning out, and it was a very heavy rainstorm. Murphy was crying and scratching at the door like crazy. I ran downstairs, and the Doc yelled out, "No, he is wet."

I turned to him and yelled back, "I don't care! This is my dog, and he is staying here or I will leave here too! How can you deny me of having my Murphy?"

The Doc always wanted to be in control of everything and every decision I made. I am sure it was his Muslim, Arabic upbringing, and he was twenty-five years my senior; but for goodness sakes, I had Murphy for eight years and he was my best friend. From that night on, Murphy lived back with us. I went over to the neighbor and explained to him that Murphy was used to being inside and close to people. I was not happy with him being left outside alone all night. The neighbor also expressed that he and his wife had split up, so it was good that we were taking him back.

After the incident with Murphy, my feelings for the Doc felt like I was on an emotional roller coaster from day to day. Everything was his way or no way. When I visited my mom, he would call there fifteen minutes after I got there and ask what time I would be back. He definitely wanted to be in control, and I knew we were headed into a tumultuous triangle.

I always loved birthdays, my birthday, my mom's birthday. I loved having something to look forward and to celebrate. Doc was the complete opposite. He loved it when I would make him a cake and buy him beautiful clothing, but when it was an occasion for me, he would not make any big deal out of it. I certainly was not expecting any diamond rings from him. He thought I had too many from Mr. Ex. He constantly told me that I spent too much money and that Mr. Ex spoiled me. I did not know the "value of the money" as he would say in his heavy Arabic accent! I would spend my paycheck from his hospital on our groceries. He would have a beautiful meal every night. I am a great cook, and he loved my food. He never offered me any money for groceries. He always complained that I would spend my paycheck too fast. The whole $184 a week I was making, it all went for groceries and for the house.

My birthday was in October, and I felt as though he sensed something was a little off with me. I was disheartened after the Murphy ordeal and realized that he was quite selfish. I also knew he was brought up that way and it was part of his Arabic culture. The men call the shots, and the women have to obey the men. He knew in his heart that this was not working for me. I would fight back on every single issue. We would go back and forth on such trivial nonsense. It all came down to money. He never spent a dime! I spent everything I had and enjoyed every penny I made. He did not like the way I handled money at all. At the time and to this day, he was never going to change me. One thing Mr. Ex taught me was to be a giving person, in every way, your kindness, love, and money, whatever it took. He definitely taught me how to give.

Once again, I came from a very humble background. I never had new clothes growing up. I wore my two sister's hand-me-downs. When my dad moved my brother and I up to Vermont to the chicken farm, I had one pair of jeans that I washed and wore every day. My oldest sister that lived in Massachusetts would give me a couple of her old shirts when we would visit. She always bought nice tops. Her pants were too big for me. I was still a kid in the beginning of my high school years. My father bought me nothing, as hard as I worked shoveling tons of manure every seven weeks. When the chickens would go to processing, he would not buy me a pair of Levi's at the local town store for $11. I was up there from ninth grade until graduation and always wore the same pair of jeans. My mom had bought me one other pair of brown pants that I wore as well. I had two pairs of pants throughout my high school years. When I met Mr. Ex, after my high school years, I had moved back to Troy. I was waiting for my best friend Gail to come out of work from his factory. He saw me and asked if I was there for a job. I told him my mom told me never to work in a sweat shop. The next day, he was at Gail's house and we were going out for Chinese food. Within one week, we were in NYC and he was buying me a new wardrobe complete with my choice of Gucci handbag and Rolex watch!

It is amazing how our lives can change overnight by just meeting someone. Needless to say, he had won me over because no man had ever bought me anything. Mr. Ex did buy me everything and anything from Porches to Mercedes to whatever I wanted. It was quite a life change for a little girl that was shoveling out a barn that contained 38,000 chickens every seven weeks. It was very easy for me to fall in love and be overwhelmed by him. He gave money to everyone, including the homeless people on the streets of NYC. He was the most generous man I had ever met to this day in my life.

The Doc saw all the clothing I brought to his house. He had to build two twenty-foot bars to connect up in the basement of his house so I could hang up my clothing. He would constantly remind me that Mr. Ex ruined me and never taught me the value of a dollar. It was okay with him when I would bring home nice sweaters and clothing for him though. He never complained and always told me that I knew good quality.

My birthday was in October, so in August, he asked me what I wanted for my birthday. I told him I wanted to go to Florence, Italy. He laughed, and I walked away. The next day, he asked me again and I repeated the same. Finally, he agreed that he would call the travel agent and arrange a trip to Florence for my birthday. That he did. There was no such thing as Expedia or a million travel sites in the late eighties. Everything was done with a travel agent. He assured me a week later that we were going to Rome and to Florence and that was my birthday present. I should not think I am getting anything else. I used to laugh at his comments because I really didn't care. He paid the bills in the house and I had my paycheck, and I was secure with that. At the time, I had a piece of land for sale, around forty-two acres in Eastport that I had a buyer for. I knew I would have a large sum of money within the next few months. Mr. Ex had bought that property for me a few years before in hopes that we would build a house on it someday. The land was in my name only. I knew I would have plenty of spending money when we went to Italy because I knew he never spent a nickel on anything. I was not used to living that way anymore, and I never wanted to live like that. He made good money with the animal hospital. If I would not have lived with him and cooked, he would have been happy to eat lentils and rice every day just so he did not have to spend any money.

His biggest complaint about me until the day he died was the way I spent money. The irony of my entire book is that it was his money that he was killed for! All of his savings had wrote him a painful death sentence.

We flew to Italy two days before my birthday. We landed in Rome and took a puddle jumper to Florence. When I ever got to the hotel, I thought someone had rented us a closet! The room was so small that you could hardly move. It was obvious that he had instructed the travel agent to get us the cheapest room. I was used to staying at the Plaza or Pierre in NYC with excellent room service. I could not believe that he was satisfied with our accommodations. I kept my mouth shut as I was happy to be with him. He did take me to see the Art in Florence for my birthday as I had requested. We were also going to spend the last two days in Rome so I could see the Sistine Chapel.

We flew to Italy a few days before my birthday. We were in Florence for my birthday. He left a small card on the bathroom shelf the day of my birthday, in Florence. I opened the card, and it had looked like something that came out of a box. It was not romantic, and I do not think it even said *love*. I specifically remember that he did not even lick the envelope closed. The top of the enveloped was just tucked in. Needless to say, I was less than impressed. I did thank him, and he kept reminding me that the trip to Italy was my birthday present! There was nothing in the card, and I was a little surprised. Florence has some of the best shopping in the world. Beautiful leather handbags and shoes were displayed in the windows of all the fine shops. It was a shopper's paradise! I was thrilled to be there. I had a few thousand dollars with me that I knew I was going to spend very quickly. As we walked around Florence the first day, he continually remarked at everything I bought and how I have "no respect" for "the money." It was a constant badgering that I was truly getting tired of hearing. It was my birthday and my money I was spending! He never let up for a minute. By the time we got back to the hotel, he had already decided that we were going to the least expensive restaurant that was near our hotel. That was fine with me. At this point, I was so pissed off, and he was actually ruining what should have been a wonderful time. All for the love of money! We went to the restaurant, and I immediately ordered a glass of wine. By the end of the meal, I drank at least three glasses of wine. He sat there very quiet, and I knew he was mad because I had drunk three glasses of wine. I really did not care at that point. I knew at that time that our relationship was never going to grow due to his constant bitching about "the money, the money," and I was supposedly the one obsessed with it? We went back to the room, and he proceeded to berate me about drinking too much wine. I finally had the chutzpah to tell him that I was so sick of listening to him complain about the money, the money! I ran out of the tiny little room and slammed the door! I went right back to the little restaurant that we had dinner in, and the matron was happy to serve me. I ordered another glass of wine, and I knew that the wait staff there could sense my sadness. They had all observed us at dinner and could see that I was not happy! This was not the happy birthday that I thought it would be. I went back to the room a few hours later, and he was out of his mind! "Where were you? I didn't know if you were hurt, and I was so worried," he went on and on. He was so mad at me, but I really did not care. His pettiness with the whole "money" thing really got to me. I was not used to being treated and tongue whipped like I was some spoiled ungrateful child. I knew in my heart that I was good to this man. I loved him with all my heart and soul. After I had received the payment from the land, I made his home beautiful—oriental rugs, expensive linens, and plenty of beautiful clothing for him. How dare he treat me like I was some kind of ingrate! I cooked and cleaned our house daily. I planted a vegetable garden for him that was at least a half acre. I tended to that garden every day. I made him fresh raspberry jam, over one hundred jars, so he could have a stockpile.

He would get mad when I gave a visitor a jar of the jam in fear that he would run out soon! He loved everything that I had done to his home, garden, wardrobe, bedroom, and life. He loved it all as long as I was not spending *his* money. As long as it was my money, I could do anything to the house I wanted. I also painted the entire interior of the house to make it feel like a home. How dare he ruin my birthday with his petty complaints about money that never stopped!

By the time our trip was finished in Rome and we had seen the Sistine Chapel, I had spent every dime I had. The money I spent was not on things only for me. The money was spent on gifts for my mom, dad, Heather, my sisters, and my brother; and certainly, plenty was spent on him. He never purchased anything for himself. He loved everything I had bought for him. He would laugh watching me trying to pack my suitcase with all the new editions. The day before we left Rome, I asked him if I could borrow a few hundred dollars until we got home. He knew I had plenty of money in the bank and knew I would pay him back. He flatly refused to give me a dime. He had a wallet full of $100 bills that he guarded and never spent. I now knew that this relationship was going to be an uphill battle. The old expression that "you truly do not know someone until you live with them" came to mind.

My birthday trip certainly made me wonder where this relationship was going. I did not have fun with him. I did enjoy the beautiful artwork of Florence and Rome. However, his constant nagging about money took away all the magic that I had imagined from this trip. I was happy to go home. I had seen a side of him that *no* woman had ever experienced personally as I did. He purported himself out to be a lover of the finer things in life, yet he had no clue as to what the actual "giving of yourself" entailed. He talked a good game to everyone. His own selfishness, when it came to money, was something to this day I will never understand.

CHAPTER 6

The Women

After my birthday had passed in October, the holidays were only weeks away. I prepared a beautiful Thanksgiving dinner for my parents and my sister and her family. I made it a small gathering as to not overwhelm him. He was not a giving person. At the animal hospital, he was very kind to people and animals. As far as giving of himself or his money, that was out of the question. I truly hated this quality in him and vowed to change it.

After Thanksgiving, I told him that I wanted to go back to college and finish my bachelor's degree. The state college was only five miles from our home. I had my associate's degree, and it would take me less than two years to get my bachelor's. He thought it was a very good idea. He asked about how much money it would cost. I told him not to worry about it. I had the money in my bank account. I enrolled for the January semester.

Christmas was coming, and I was happy to go back to college after the New Year. It would give me a different focus and get me out of the house more. My days were spent cleaning, cooking, and working at his animal hospital. Basically, my entire existence was centered around the Doc and his needs.

I love Christmas! I went out and bought a beautiful big tree. I had it all set up with bright lights and ornaments before he came home from the hospital that day. When he walked in the house, I had plugged in the lights and the room was magical! The tree was spectacular! A big smile came across his face, and I knew in my heart that he had never had a Christmas tree like this before, decorated with love!

He complimented me and spoke of how beautiful the tree was. He also reminded me that he was a Muslim and they do not celebrate Christmas. I told him that was fine. Mr. Ex was Jewish yet we still had a tree every year and celebrated both Christmas and Chanukah.

As the days counted down to Christmas, I continued to place packages for my family and for the Doc under the tree. About a week before Christmas, he asked me what I wanted. I exclaimed, "Surprise me!" I was hoping for an engagement ring. I still loved him very much and wanted to be his wife and have his children. The next day, he took $200 out of his wallet and told me to go buy something for Christmas as he was "not good at these things." I was a little surprised as he had never handed me money before. I thought this was a distraction because he was going to get me a ring and did not want me to think he was!

Somehow, living day to day with him was enjoyable at times because we were both preoccupied with work. He was a good man. I am not trying to make him out to be a bad person. He was just very, very selfish when it came to money, and he did not know how to give easily as I had been taught by Mr. Ex. I loved him dearly and knew in my heart that he would change. Once he realized that my love for him would make him happier than any money could, things would be different. I knew this was going to take some time.

The next day was Christmas. I was so excited. I was so happy! I had bought him a beautiful silk robe, a few Ralph Lauren sweaters, and down jacket, and many, many more beautiful gifts. The tree was full of packages. He would come home at night and sit and drink his tea and stare at the tree.

On Christmas Eve, I went to my mom's alone as he continued telling me how he does not celebrate Christmas. That was okay with me. He had his ways. I brought my mom and dad their gifts as well as my sisters and brother and their children. I always loved to watch their kids at Christmas open the gifts I had gotten them. My family knew that the Doc was a Muslim, and they were not at all offended that he did not come with me for our yearly ritual. My mom's cooking and opening presents were my favorite time of year with my family. Both my sisters had bought him a gift and so did my mom. My mom and I hugged and laughed, and she also thought that he was going to surprise me with an engagement ring or ask me to marry him. I was very happy.

I left my mom's at about eight thirty and called to tell him I was on my way home. When I got back home, he was sitting and staring at the tree. I had the gifts from my sisters and brother and my mom and dad for him. He said, "What is that for?" I laughed and said it was their Christmas presents to him. He continued to say that he did not celebrate Christmas and they should not buy him anything. I laughed and told him that I had bought them plenty and they were very grateful that he was in my life.

I told him it was time for him to open his presents. I explained to him that my family always opened our presents on Christmas Eve, even when we were kids. My mom would wake us up at twelve midnight to tell us that Santa had come! Those were the happiest days of my life.

He began opening his presents. I handed him each one and told him that I knew he was going to love each one better than the next! He laughed and continued opening. He loved the silk robe! He loved everything! No one had ever showered him with Christmas gifts as I did. By the time he was finished, it was almost midnight. We had laughed while he was opening gifts and had some of my mom's food. I kept looking at the clock thinking, "He will wait until midnight, until it is Christmas, to surprise me with a ring." The clock struck midnight as my big grandfather clock echoed through the house. He sat there quietly, and I sat there quietly. He said he was tired and was going to bed. I laughed to myself and thought surely he was going to where ever he hid the ring to get it and surprise me!

I sat staring at the glowing lights on the Christmas tree waiting for him to come back to the living room. The minutes turned into hours and warm tears started streaming down my cheeks. My heart sunk into my chest. I felt lifeless. There was no ring. There were no gifts. There was nothing for me. I cried myself to sleep in the chair as he laid sleeping in the bed on Christmas Eve.

I woke up in the chair about five in the morning still with the hopes that maybe there would be a surprise for me today, on Christmas Day. He walked out of the bedroom and looked at my face. It was obvious I had been crying, and I was an empty shell.

He said, "What's wrong with you?"

I replied, "Nothing."

I had to get out of that house. I had to scream my lungs out because I was so hurt. I didn't know what to do. I told him I was going to the animal hospital to take care of the animals left there over Christmas. I took Murphy, and we left in a hurry. I could not look at him. I did not want to be around him. I was so hurt. Not even one present for me to open? Why? To this day, I will never understand. I never said a word to him, but he knew I was now a completely different girl. I felt like a wounded bird that had been left to die. There was no rhyme or reason for him not getting me a gift, even if it wasn't a ring. The religion talk and being a Muslim did not stop him from opening his beautiful gifts. I was beyond hurt.

I drove to my mom's after caring for the animals at the hospital. I waited for my dad to go out. She held me as I cried my eyes out, and she had no explanation to give me. She was very upset that he had not even given me any type of gift. She knew that our tree was full of beautiful gifts for him. She could not understand how he could hurt me like that.

After the horrible Christmas experience, I was a different person. Things he had done all the time now began to irritate the hell out of me. From the time I had moved in with him, some eight months before until now, various women would call our house at night. The calls came at least three times a week from women I became very familiar with. One was the next-door neighbor's wife. I called her the drunken redhead! She would get drunk all the time, and he would sit on the phone with her listening and talking for an hour. Then, there was the heavy school teacher that he had a long-term affair with (according to my best sources close to him, i.e., Heather). Heather knew every woman that he had an affair with. She would show me how he marked their cards N/C. At the animal hospital, that meant no charge! There were lots of N/Cs, but there were also the very few discreet affairs that he did not want anyone to know about. Unfortunately, when they called our house and I knew their name, it was very easy to connect the dots! To this day, I have never told one of my dearest friends, Dr. Gardener, that his now ex-wife was among the loyal group of the Sheikh's Harem!

I started college in January and worked at the hospital as well. I studied, worked, and took care of the Doc, the house, and the garden in springtime. You name it. I did it all! I was so involved with my studies that I overlooked the nonsense of his phone calls. One particular night, I was very tired and had a test the next day. The phone rang about ten in the evening, and I answered. It was the drunken redhead!

She said, "Let me talk to Doc."

I was so pissed. I said, "I do not want you calling here anymore!"

"How would you like me to call your husband late at night?"

I hung up the phone.

He came running up the stairs and said, "Who was that?"

I said, "It was the drunken redhead you have been screwing without her husband knowing. I am sick and tired of her calling here."

He flipped out! "She is one of my clients."

"Bullshit," I exclaimed. "Don't ever try to convince me you have not had affairs with these women! I am so sick and tired of these calls and these women! How would you like it if I had three to four different men calling me here?"

He was so mad at me. He did not talk to me for two weeks. I didn't care. I was nobody's fool, and "the women" were not my friends. They were his ex-lovers or affairs or whatever! The next day, I went into the local market and I saw the redhead. She was in line right in front of me. She cashed out and hurried out the door. I cashed out quickly and ran out the door and over to her car.

I said, "Hey, Susie, don't call my house! As long as I live there, I do not want you calling there. Do you understand me? Otherwise, I will go see your husband that works nights and let him know how you get drunk and call the doc every week."

She raced out of the parking lot, and I knew she was going to go home and call the Doc. We could see her house from our bedroom window. No sooner did I get home, her car was in her driveway and the Doc was in the front yard waiting for me.

"What are you a crazy woman?" he asked.

"Crazy as a fox," I said. I was mad as hell! I walked into the house and ignored him completely. I told him he had better not open his mouth to me! "I was not stupid, and there is no reason for this woman or any of the other women to be calling here and speaking to you on the phone for hours unless you were sleeping with them or you still are!"

Three weeks went by, and he never spoke a word to me. I could have cared less. I studied at night and went to school in the mornings and the animal hospital in the afternoons. I carried on my days as if nothing happened, but the phone calls finally stopped. Apparently, he heard my message loud and clear. He knew I was ready to leave him if he continued to treat me like a second-class citizen that had no say in a home that was supposed to be mine. He always told me that it was my home. Well, I did not want these nefarious woman calling *my* house!

On Thursdays, the animal hospital was closed. He had the whole day off. The first year, he would stay home and garden or do paperwork in his home office. After the second year, he would disappear from eight in the morning until nine in the evening. One evening, I had made a nice dinner and sat there waiting for him to come home. His Audi pulled in around nine in the evening. I ran down to the door outraged.

"Where have you been? You have been gone all day and night."

He looked at me and said, "I don't answer to any woman."

I said, "Well, I guess it is time for me to move out! You have no respect for me, and you are lying to me."

He did not expect me to say that!

I had just learned that afternoon that my mom had very bad ovarian cancer. She had been hiding the illness from me for the past year and a half. She could not hide it anymore as her pain was excruciating.

Why was I wasting my time with a man that has no feelings? He can do whatever he wants, and I am just his housekeeper and cook? I knew my mom needed me, and I wanted to be there for her. She was very sick. We had spoken the day before. She said she would love for me to come and live with her and my dad to help. My father was beside himself. He did not know how to handle any of this. Neither did I, but I needed to help my mom more than I wanted to fight with the Doc about his comings and goings and lies.

I never questioned the fact that he loved me. It was the cultural differences that we could not seem to agree upon. He was eighteen years my senior, an Egyptian Muslim veterinarian, and a confirmed bachelor. He told me he never wanted to be married. I wanted a husband and children. I was twenty-six years old. My mom would always say, "Why buy the cow when you can get the milk for free!" He was so worried about anyone touching *his* money as well. I knew I had to leave and take care of my mother. After the second Christmas with *no* gift for me, that was the icing on the cake.

I was graduating in May with my bachelor's degree and high honors. I also needed my job at the animal hospital. I loved working there. I knew he did not believe me when I said I wanted to leave. He also now knew that my mother was dying. I had a lot on my plate, and my mom encouraged me to stay until I graduated and then make my move after that. We decided that would be the best plan for me. My dad knew that I would be coming to live with them. He adored the Doc, but he too wanted me to be married and not just living with the Doc.

The months passed, and I did very well with all my exams. I continued taking care of the house and cooking wonderful meals. He had told me that I had changed and wanted to know what was wrong with me. I finally exploded! I said, "After two Christmas with not one gift and no promise of marriage and you do not want children, what the hell am I doing here? Hire a servant like you used to have in Egypt!"

He walked away and still did not take me seriously about my leaving. I was ready to go to my mom's. She needed me, he didn't. He had lived just fine without me. He had all his lady friends that would once again call him when I left, and his life did not have to be such a big secret in his own house anymore because I would be gone.

Graduation day came. The Doc and my father took me and watched as I received my honors. My mom was much too weak and sick to attend. After I had that diploma in my hand, I wanted to go back to his house, pack, and live with my mom who was dying.

CHAPTER 7

The Angel of Death

A few days after I graduated, I was ready to move to my mom's house. I knew he would be at the animal hospital all morning. I packed up my collection of Hummels that were displayed along the tops of the cabinets in the kitchen. I left a few here and there in the house because I knew he loved looking at them. I also had a beautiful collection of Lladros that he loved. There were porcelain girls with animals and clowns that he looked at every day. He loved those Lladros. Mr. Ex had bought me all my collections, and they were all very expensive. The Doc loved them as well, but he would have never paid that sum of money for a porcelain figurine. I had a very large clown that had his arm around a little girl in the center of our dining room table. That was his favorite. Most of the figurines had animals, but they were all very expensive and very beautiful.

Once I packed all the Hummels from the tops of the kitchen cabinets, the kitchen looked stark and bare. I wanted to take my things with me. I had also hoped that he would change and we would someday make our relationship work. I was only twenty-six. I still wanted to marry him, and I still wanted his children.

My clothes were packed in the car, and the Hummels were beside them. I still had lots of stuff that I needed to move out of there. Then, there was Murphy. My dad would not let me take him to their house, especially now with my mom being so sick. I knew in my heart that the Doc would want him because Murphy always sat by his side and loved him. I was hoping he would let him stay because he had a nice big yard there and Murphy was such an obedient dog.

Twelve o'clock was coming, and I apparently had failed to realize that the Doc was coming home for lunch. He did not know I was leaving that day.

Suddenly, I heard the Audi pull in the driveway and my heart sunk and my head pounded. I now had to confront something that I never thought would end this way.

He walked upstairs to the kitchen and looked around for a minute.

I said, "Do you want tea?"

He said, "Yes."

I always had a tray of tea made for him whenever he walked through the door. I knew by his expression that he saw the Hummels gone. He paused for a minute and looked in the kitchen again.

He said, "What are you doing?"

I brought him his tray of tea, and he turned his back to me and stared out at the field. I told him that I was moving to my mom's house. I said it would be better for the both of us. I continued to speak in a soft voice. He never said a word and never turned the rotating leather chair around. I continued putting some things in boxes.

He said, "What about Murphy?"

I told him that I needed to leave Murphy with him because my mom was very sick, and my dad could not handle it anymore. Murphy was sitting by his side as he always did. I said that Murphy would be a good friend to him while I was gone. He could take him to the animal hospital every day as we always did. He would lay in the Doc's office and wait for him. The Doc still remained dead silent. I continued moving my things into the car and was ready to take my first load of things to my mom's.

I went back upstairs and said, "Talk to me. I love you. Don't you know that?"

He would not turn around. I was so upset. I walked over to his chair and spun it around toward me. His eyes were streaming with tears rolling down his cheeks, and he was crying silently and could not stop. I fell to my knees and hugged him. I started crying so hard.

This was the first time in two years that he had ever showed any sign of emotion. It was also the first time that I felt he did truly love me.

I sat on his lap, and we cried together, holding each other and crying. Neither of us could stop crying.

He said, "What do you want?"

I said, "I love you. I want to marry you. I want to have children. I want what every woman my age wants."

He said, "Please don't leave now."

I told him I would stay for a few weeks so he could think about what I wanted. After that, I would move to my mom's because she was dying and she needed me more than he did. I kissed him and told him I loved him and will always love him. I told him I would be back that night after taking care of my mom and moving some of my things.

When I left, he was still sitting there with warm tears rolling down his cheeks. My heart was broken and so was his. As hurt as I was, I still knew that something had to change. I was unhappy with the relationship the way it was and felt powerless at times. This was not healthy for either one of us.

I came back later that night, and he was very happy to see me. We laughed and joked and got along better than we ever had. It was just like old times. He knew I was hurting so badly because my mom was dying. Every day in the animal hospital, clients would ask me how my mom was. I always say she was going to get better. I always believed that.

Once two weeks went by, and he said nothing of marriage or children. I left and went to my mom's. He wanted me to stay working at the animal hospital. I was very happy about that. I still needed him in my life. I loved him, and he was still a source of strength for me and a shoulder to lean on. He knew what a wonderful lady my mother was, and he knew I needed to be there for her.

After a year went by, I knew he was living his old life again. I was not interested as my focus was on my mom. I had started running every day just to release my pain. My mom had expressed to me several times that she wished she had a little dog to keep her company when I was working. My dad worked nights. I also worked a few nights a week as a bartender to pay the bills.

One Saturday, a lovely client came in the office with a litter of seven-week-old dachshund puppies. She was selling them for $600 each with papers. The Doc was checking them out and giving them their first shots and worming. There was one pup that had a bubble on his head that she had popped, and she could not sell him for the $600 like the other pups. When she came out of the office, I took one of the puppies and said, "Oh Mary, I wish I could afford one of these for my mom." Apparently, she had asked the Doc how my mom was. He told her that my mom was dying of ovarian cancer and I was now living with her. She paid her bill and left with the puppies. We closed at one on Saturdays. At twelve forty-five, Mary called the hospital and asked me to meet her at the local restaurant as she needed to show me something. I told her I would be there as soon as I got out. We closed up, and I raced to meet her. She was already in the parking lot. She asked me to get in her car. I got in and sat down. She handed me the tiny puppy with the bubble on his head and said, "This is Lightning Bolt. At least, that is what we call him. I want you to have him for your mother." I was so elated and thankful. I hugged her and could not wait to get home to give the baby to my mom. I knew I would be taking care of the pup, but he could come with me to the beach and run every morning. My mom went crazy! Oh how she loved that little dog. She named him Sonny! Every day, Sonny and I would leave at five in the morning and run the beach so he would be dog tired when I left him with her all day. My dad was not thrilled with the new pup, but he was so little and adorable that you could not help but like him. That dog gave my mom a new reason to feel better. He also kept me in great shape. I was running four to five miles a day, and he would run in front of me chasing the seagulls on the beach!

The following week, a woman that owned the local pharmacy had come in with her cat. She was a widow and seemed very sweet. She would talk to me about her cat, and I would talk about my mom. I liked her. That day after she left, the Doc and I were alone.

I walked into his office and said, "Well, since you don't want to ever get married and you don't want any kids, why don't you call Linda, the lady that owns the pharmacy? She seemed nice enough?"

He smiled at me and said, "What do I need you to fix me up now?"

I said, "No, but she does very well and seems like a nice person, and I wish you would go out with someone that is not married!"

He laughed, but he listened to me. He called her, and they began seeing each other every Saturday night. He was a very private man, and he had promised me that there would *never* be another woman living in his house after me. This was a very true statement. Unfortunately, I did not realize at the time that I had encouraged him to be with a woman that would slowly kill him for his money. Everyone in town thought she had her own money just as I did. Everyone in town also thought she was a very nice person as she purported to be. What I did not realize at the time was that every woman does not think like me! I accepted him for the person he was. I knew he was a ladies' man. I knew he kept lots of secrets. I knew he guarded his money and it was the most important thing in his life. I also knew that after I left him, he was so hurt by my action that he wanted to see me struggle financially, even with my mother dying. I continued to work for him. He began a regular Saturday night relationship with his "angel of death." He thought she had plenty of money and loved him and was such a wonderful person. He felt very safe going out with her because he figured she would never need a dime from him. That was the perfect relationship for the Doc—a woman that had plenty of money and would never want or spend a dime of his money. This whole thought process could not have been further from the truth. A Rite Aid pharmacy opened about four miles from her little local pharmacy about eight years after their Saturday night dates continued. He never saw her during the week, and the only place he ever went with her was on her *free* pharmaceutical trips to Chicago. It cost him nothing. She was a heavy smoker and had continued to gain weight through the years. I am sure she wanted more of a relationship with him or to see him more, but he called the shots. He did not fall in love easily. He did what was convenient for him. He also never wined and dined her or anyone else. I am quite sure that I am the only woman on this earth that he paid to go on vacations with. After Italy, he did take me to the Bahamas once, but that was another disaster. His constant complaining about money was such a turnoff. He never showed this side of himself to Linda, his angel of death. He figured she was rich in her own right and needed nothing from him. Little did he know!

His longtime friend and real estate agent, Mike, called him from Florida about a great investment property that he could buy very cheap. He trusted Mike. He flew down to Florida and bought the three-bedroom condo for cash. I always knew he was tired of the cold winters in Connecticut. Now, he had a place to go and a reason to take a vacation. He never went anywhere, except to Egypt every eight years and the few places we had gone. It was quite a few years before he accepted Linda's invitation for her free trips.

During the next year, my mom had died two weeks before Christmas. I stayed in the hospital with her every night and slept on a cart. I was devastated. I started running more and more every day. The April after she died, I ran my first New York marathon in her honor. I placed the white gauze gloves that they had put on her arms in the hospital around my wrists. I finished the marathon in three hours and twenty minutes.

The following day, I went to the animal hospital and the Doc said he was very proud of me. That made me feel really good. He knew at the time that I had started going out with another Jewish man. I had met him six years earlier before the Doc. I had dinner with him a few times. I never pursued a relationship with him because he too was married—Mr. Johnny NY! He was the most successful retailer on the east coast! Boy, I could attract them! It must have been my shiksappeal!

The Doc never said anything to me about him, and I always spoke very highly of him. He knew who he was and also knew that he was a very successful man. Johnny NY was there with me when my mom died and was a great comfort to me, but my heart still loved the Doc.

CHAPTER 8

The Final Straw

During the next several months, my relationship with Johnny NY was great. My dad had let me rent the apartment underneath him, and I still helped him with cooking and cleaning as my mom had passed. I continued running daily and was in the best shape of my life. At times, I would joke with the Doc and ask him how his relationship was with Linda. He would say, "I only see her once a week. That is enough." I would laugh because I knew in my heart there were plenty of other women in his life. I am sure they were all married because he did not buy presents and did not want any obligations to any woman. He had Murphy, and he had his new condo in Florida near his old friend Mike. He started taking vacations to Florida, and according to Heather, he had an absolutely gorgeous condo. A lady from France had decorated and designed the condo and had to go back to France in a hurry. Mike got him an incredible deal in a real upscale part of Florida, something he would have never purchased. Mike was a flashy guy and always drove a Rolls-Royce. He made his money selling real estate out of the trunk of that Rolls-Royce after he had sold the plaza that the Doc's hospital was in. He parled 600K into millions, and the Doc admired him for his business savvy. Doc now started going back and forth to Florida three to four times that year.

In late September of that year, my dad was rushed to Mass General for open heart surgery and was near death's door. It was a Saturday at the hospital, and I was anxious to get out so I could drive to Boston to visit him. The Doc used to give me an extra $20 a month if I bleached and waxed all the floors in the animal hospital every month on a Saturday. I told him I had to leave too because I had a long drive. My dad was in very bad shape. He insisted that I stay at the hospital and wash the floors! I flipped out completely! I took the key of the animal hospital off my clip after seven years and threw it at him!

"You son of a bitch. My father is dying, and all you are interested in is me washing your damn floors for $20? Go to hell and wash your own damn floors."

It was all a control thing with him. He now realized he had lost control of me. I had a new man in my life that was very good to me. He resented me once again because my new beau was well off and he knew that Johnny NY was sitting in the funeral home when he attended my mother's wake. He knew Johnny NY really cared about me, and he knew he was about to lose me for good. He was in shock when I handed him the key.

He said, "You will never get it back."

I said, "Good, because you are a heartless bastard, and all you care about is what you want, not what is important to me."

I ran out the door crying my eyes out and thinking about my father. I was hoping he would still be alive by the time I reached the hospital.

My dad came home about a week later and was very sore but getting around. I was unemployed and very poor. I never said a word to Johnny NY because I was too proud as my mom had taught me. I called my friend at the family restaurant, and he offered to let me bartend again on two nights so I could pay my dad the rent. Four days before my birthday, Johnny NY and I were downstairs watching a movie. It was about twelve midnight. I heard a banging on the floor from upstairs. I got the key to upstairs and ran up to find my dad had an aneurysm burst and blood was pouring out of his mouth as he said, "Do not resuscitate me!" I was crying and called 911. My sister came running from next door, and the ambulance came. He died at the house, but we followed the ambulance to the hospital and waited in the waiting room. I was still hoping he would be okay. The doctor called me in and told me that he had died! Ten months after my mom had just died! I was a train wreck! Johnny NY drove me back home and stayed with me. Our bond was now growing as he was there with me for both the death of my mom and my dad.

The Doc never attended my dad's wake, but he did have Heather send a beautiful spray of flowers. My dad really liked the Doc and used to go to our house and help him with his garden. He planted climbing roses on a fence for him. I remember because the Doc ripped all the roses out after I moved out! He wanted no memories of my beautiful garden because he was so mad that I had left him. He had no control over me anymore.

Every now and then, I would go in the animal hospital to see Heather, and he would call me in his office and ask me how I was doing. I always responded that I was doing very well. I had rented a big house in the most exclusive area of Eastport after my father died. Johnny NY moved in with me. It was a beautiful big home and decorated nicely.

The Doc had met Johnny NY as I took him in the animal hospital to meet him. I always wanted his approval. He liked him very much. That year, we invited the Doc to our rented home for Passover. I knew he loved my cooking, and he showed up for dinner in a great mood. I asked him why he did not bring Linda with him. He said, "No, I don't want her here." He still loved me. I knew he did. He also knew that he was very welcome in my home and that Johnny NY was very sincere and liked the Doc very much. We always had a feast, and I always sent him home with lots of my food. He loved that. I was always sad to see him go because I knew he was going home to an empty house, but he still had Murphy. Linda was of no consequence. She never knew he was coming to my house for dinner because he never told her.

The same year my father died, Johnny NY's mom died and he came into a good deal of money. We bought 3.5 acres of land up the road. It had a beautiful view of the river, and he wanted me to build my dream house.

CHAPTER 9

Our Newfound Love

I always wanted to believe in my heart that the Doc was happy for me. I also always found a way to continue seeing him regularly. When my mom died, I kept her little dog Sonny. I took him to the animal hospital to see the Doc all the time. He knew the dog reminded me of my mother. He knew I loved that dog. To this day, I still have a Sonny. My mom's Sonny died at twenty-three years old, and I got another one less than a week later. Doc was now seeing things about me that he never took the time to see before. He was realizing how much he meant to me as a person, no matter what he did. I did not care about the other women. I did not care who he slept with. All I cared about was trying to make him understand that real love between two people never dies. He now knew I loved him with all my heart, and I knew he truly loved me.

After Passover, Johnny NY asked me to marry him and gave me a beautiful emerald ring. He bought the 3.5-acre lot overlooking the Eastport river and put it in my name and handed me the deed. I was about to become his third wife. He was twenty-three years my senior, but that never occurred to me. He loved me, and I knew it. He accepted me through all of my craziness and when my parents died, and he also knew that I had lived with the Doc. He welcomed him with open arms in our home. Johnny NY also knew that the Doc loved me very much. He was never intimidated by any other man. He was confident and successful. He worked seven days a week, and his father was a legend in the small town next to Eastport because of his department store. The store was in business for eighty-five years. People would say he was the richest man in town, and at one time, he was.

I started working in my fiancé's stores every day. We did very well. One day, he surprised me and brought home a brand-new Land Rover for me! I had been driving a Volkswagen Jetta for the past three years. As much as I was still in deep mourning about the death of my parents, Johnny NY was determined to do whatever it took to get my mind off my pain and sorrow and help me heal my heart. I couldn't wait to show Heather my new car! I drove straight over to the animal hospital and made her and the Doc come outside. The truck was the classic dark green with all the bells and whistles, and boy, was it pretty! Heather loved it, and for the first time in his life, he was actually happy to see me smile again. The past few years, I had been so down because of my mom and dad's untimely deaths. I went in the office and showed him the deed to the land Johnny NY had given to me. "He wants me to build my dream house," I exclaimed. The Doc didn't know how to react and could not believe how this man was so generous to me in such a short time. I carried on and told him that Johnny NY knows a great woman when he finds one! I said it jokingly, but I knew he was feeling like he had now lost me forever. As far as marriage and children, he never wanted that from me. Even if he did, which I know to this day he wished he would have, there was no chance of it happening now. He loved me, but he resented me for leaving him. Until his last days, he would never forgive me for leaving him, but he would always love me more than any woman he had ever loved. I knew that and I know that today.

He would always be a part of my life. Every week, I would stop in the animal hospital to see him. I would bring him clothing from our stores. I would bring him food that I made. He loved when I made Egyptian food. I would still make it especially for him.

The house was finally finished after a year. It was incredible. Southern yellow pine floors throughout, four different Italian-tiled bathrooms, three fireplaces, and a wood stove, it was exquisite.

I had made a list of people that I would invite for my house-warming party. Some were friends that I had met through the

Doc that lived right across the street from me. The house was in a very exclusive area, and we spared no costs. It was magnificent! Hand-painted murals graced the walls and fifty-three windows with exquisite window treatments on every one. Ethan Allen furniture in every room, and every room had its own little theme. Our bedroom was fifty by twenty on the top floor with a panoramic view of the Eastport river. Johnny NY was so proud of what I had created. He knew I was there six times a day with the carpenters. Everything was handpicked by me, from the tile to the doorknobs to the color of every fabric. He wanted a house-warming party because he was so proud of our new home!

I made a list of around twenty people, which included the Doc and Linda. At that time, Linda was attractive and kept her hair blond, and she was about a size 10. I went to the animal hospital and begged him to come and bring Linda. I was so proud of my house, and I had finally felt that I had accomplished so many things to be proud of. After going back and forth with him, he finally agreed that he would bring Linda to my house-warming party. I really wanted Johnny NY to meet her because my thoughts about her had changed drastically. I had come to realize that this supposedly wealthy woman wore cheap clothes and carried a fake Coach bag and really had no class at all. My soon-to-be husband was a great judge of character, and I knew he would tell it like he saw it! I loved that quality about him. If he thought someone had no class, he would immediately identify their bad behavior.

Linda was pretty some fifteen years ago when I had my house warming party, but she always dressed provocatively, something I never did. She wore cheap dresses and cheap perfume. I was beginning to understand why the Doc did not take her out in public at all.

The party was formal, but the men were not required to wear a tux, just a jacket. The woman came in beautiful dresses, and I had on a beautiful simple black dress as always. Linda walked in with a very low-cut dress with half her boobs hanging out and some type of cheap outdated bolero over it! She looked like a hooker! She was an attractive blond at the time, so naturally, the men were drawn to her. I watched doc as he mingled with some of our old friends and how he completely ignored her. I had a table full of wines and appetizers that were exceptional. Within ten minutes, she walked over to me and asked me for Southern Comfort. I apologized and told her that I did not serve hard liquor at my home. I explained to her that there were some wonderful wines from France and Italy, but she had no interest. She wanted Southern Comfort! I sent a friend of mine to the local liquor store to accommodate her request. She downed four or five Southern Comfort drinks on ice in less than an hour. We were all having a good time, and the party was a great success. I knew that all my lady friends there could not get over her hooker-like clothing and were bewildered that the Doc would be with such a harlot. I had never seen her in a social situation or party before, so this was a real eye-opener for me. I now understood why he did not want to take her anywhere or bring her to my home for holiday meals. As my mom used to say, "You can't make a silk purse out of a sow's ear." Apparently, her supposed money could not buy her class either.

Much to my surprise, after everyone left, Johnny NY came to me and said he did not believe what she did to him.

I said, "What what?"

He said she had quite the buzz on, and as she was talking to him, she pushed her knee into his crotch and started rubbing her leg against him!

I said, "You have got to be kidding me."

He was dead serious! He said, "What does he see in that broad? I hope he is not serious about her?"

I explained to him that he had been seeing her for many years on Saturday night only, and I knew that he would never live with her or marry her.

"Thank God for that," he exclaimed.

Needless to say, my future husband was not at all impressed by this so-called wealthy local business woman. He thought she was, as he put it, "a fucking idiot." He considered her an embarrassment to the Doc, but he also observed that the Doc stayed far away from her the entire night as she got drunk. He knew that the Doc could not have possibly been in love with Linda just by his watching the both of them over the course of the evening. In a way, it made me happy because I too felt that she cheapened him, no matter what he did privately. She was an embarrassment, and she did not know how to dress like a lady. She looked real cheap!

Heather was there, and she also was offended by Linda and could not get over her hooker-like dress with half her breasts hanging out. The way she was hanging all over the men, no woman at my home was impressed by this mess in a dress! Talk about white trash!

A few months after the party, I had adopted two puppies from the local shelter. Naturally, I went in to see the Doc. He was happy to see me but scolded me about getting too many dogs. I already had my mom's dog and now two more. I would always laugh and tell him I was getting more because I had just fenced in the 3.5 acres. We laughed together, and he never spoke about her. He never mentioned her ever. I assumed she was still his Saturday night lay and that was all. Heather had told me that he had complained to her that all Linda wanted was sex all the time, and he could not stand that. I am sure he tolerated it because everything was on his terms. She did not live with him, and he had no intention of marrying her. Heather knew that better than anyone. She had spent every day working with him for over thirty years! She knew him like a book. She also knew that he still had his phone calls and the N/C women (no charge) at the office. The Doc was loyal to himself and himself only. He did what he wanted to do, and no woman was going to tell him differently.

I am sure after all the years Linda had been seeing him, she resented the hell out of him because she had to know that there were other women. She wanted everyone in town to think that he was her boyfriend and he played her game.

A year after the house was built, we got married by a rabbi in a small ceremony. I went to the animal hospital and showed him my beautiful diamond wedding band, and he knew I was very happy. I was running many of our stores now, and we were both working very hard. My husband and I were making excellent money, and life was good. I continued to get more dogs and then built a barn and got a few horses. I had always loved to ride. I built my own private dressage arena and had instructors coming to my house. I was always doing something new. I travelled to Australia, and I would call home and call the Doc. He would always be fascinated how I went everywhere and anywhere. I remember taking my niece to South Africa and calling him almost every other day to ask him what he wanted me to bring back for him. I always bought him beautiful gifts and never went anywhere without bringing him something special. I continued to cook Egyptian food for him and bring him containers. He would freeze the food so he would have it. He came to our house at least four to five times a year for holiday meals, either the Jewish holidays or catholic. He never brought Linda back to my home after the house-warming party. He never talked about her to me. It was as if she were nonexistent.

CHAPTER 10

Munchausen Syndrome

The years rolled by, and the Doc and I saw each other all the time. I had ten dogs, two horses, and a pet Llama. He would come to the house to give the horses their shots. I would always have something special for him—a new Paul and Shark sweater and a big container of lentils and rice spiced with fresh cumin. He loved coming to my home. He could not believe what I had built overlooking the river. He would sit in my overstuffed chair, drink his tea, and tell me what a lucky girl I was. I guess I was. I still never had children, and to this day, that left an empty hole in my heart. The dogs made up for it. My time was spent working and taking care of all my animals. He could never understand how and why I would spend so much time and money on all these animals. He would always tell me that I had too many. When I would adopt a new pup, I would call him at home and tell him I needed to see him right away. I would always sound sad. He would tell me to come right over. I would create these sad stories about how I found the puppy in a dumpster, and he would immediately hug the puppy and tell him that he was a "good guy." He loved all my dogs, and they loved him. He still had Murphy, and he loved him. The Doc took Murphy to work with him every day, and Murphy was his best friend.

After many years of flying back and forth to Florida, he had told me that he was getting very tired of it. He wanted to close the animal hospital after thirty years and retire. He had definitely worked very hard for thirty years. I was very surprised that he wanted to sell his condo in Florida. We got into a conversation, and finally, the truth came out. He loved living in Eastport, and that was where his permanent residence was. That was where he purchased his plot at High Valley Cemetery some forty years beforehand. Heather and he had bought their plots at the same time for very little money some forty years ago. They were side by side. I kept encouraging him to keep the condo. The winters were cold in Eastport, and as he got older, Florida would be nice for him in the winter. Finally, the truth came out! He informed me that Linda did not want him going to Florida anymore because she suspected he had a girlfriend there, which I am sure he did. Apparently, after spending the last sixteen years on Saturday night at her house, she had gained some influence over his decision making. He did not want to be alone all the time when he was in Eastport, and she did not cost him a dime. He always hated spending any money, so the plane fares were probably annoying him as well. He had plenty saved and never spent a dime. He told me that he was going to drive down to the condo because he had taken some of my Lladros down there and he wanted to drive them back as he did not want them broken. He told me that he had my clowns in the condo. I had never seen the condo, nor was I invited. I was married, and I knew he did not want to interfere with my success and new life.

The following February, he drove down to Florida because he finally sold the place for real big money. He paid sixty thousand and sold it for 460K. Nice profit! While he was driving back from Florida, he got into an automobile accident and was hospitalized. I knew nothing of this until a month later when he told me. I had visited him at his house and asked him where his car was. He said it was totaled and he was not getting another. He always had a pickup truck as well and felt much safer in the truck.

Apparently, Linda had to fly down there when he was hospitalized. He was only in the hospital a few days, so I did not suspect it was very serious. He was glad to be back in Eastport with the condo sold, and he did not have to listen to the nagging from Linda about his Florida girlfriend. (I have a very good idea who she was, and she was a beautiful Egyptian girl that was once married to a friend of his.) He never told his secrets, but the fact that he mentioned to me that she

60

was now living in Florida and divorced from his ex-friend, I pretty much summarized what was going on. She was a lovely woman, but she had two children from her previous marriage. I am sure she was a great comfort to him when he was in Florida. She spoke Arabic and understood his ways.

I never went to Linda's pharmacy as I did not think much of her anymore. She certainly was not improving the Doc's life in any way. He would never marry her or live with her. I knew that, and I am sure she knew that. I am also sure that she knew he communicated with me all the time and also with other women. I am sure her resentment toward him was deep seated and relentless. There was nothing she was ever going to say or do to change him. I would think that after seeing someone for sixteen years that if you are not married to them or living with them, it's not going to happen. This was the obvious! Even Heather would always say to me, he will never marry her or live with her. We all knew it. He was retiring and definitely a confirmed bachelor. He never went anywhere publicly with Linda; she was an embarrassment. The clothing alone looked like it was from Frederick's of Hollywood! Unfortunately, everything she wore was of cheap quality, but she drove a Mercedes. I guess she thought that was the icon of success!

About six months after he closed the animal hospital, and his accident in Florida, he seemed to be having some very bad swelling problems with his legs. I went over to his house all the time to bring food or one of the dogs. I noticed his legs were so swollen.

I said, "My god, what is wrong with your legs? They are so full of fluid."

He claimed that his legs were a result of the car accident he had in Florida, which made no sense to me. After all, he was now seeing Linda a little more and she owned a pharmacy. She was giving him all the medical advice he needed. She graduated from high school! She was not a pharmacist and not a medical doctor and never encouraged him to go to a good doctor! However, she did have access to any drug on the market as she owned the local pharmacy!

In the first year, it never occurred to me that she would intentionally poison him or crush up some type of cancer pill and put it in his Saturday night cake. Heather and I would laugh about this because Heather was the one that told me she makes him a cake every Saturday night. After almost two years and seeing him wearing orthopedic shoes from her pharmacy with the toes cut out, I was livid! His legs were so swollen. He could hardly walk.

"Why aren't you going to a doctor? You are retaining so much fluid in your legs that you can hardly walk."

He would get mad at me and say, "Don't worry. It will go down."

Apparently, Dr. Death (Linda) was giving him her home brew remedy that certainly was not curing his ailments. He was in so much pain. He could hardly walk or get up. I started noticing cheap little flower arrangements in his house, which only told me that she was now coming to his house. This was unusual. For the first fourteen years, she never went near that house due to the fact that it was still a place he slept with me. She was still jealous of our relationship. He never wanted to live with her. He liked his own house and wanted to stay there, and he told me that she hated his house.

I always passed my little comments about the cheap flower arrangements, and I was sure that Linda put them there. He would have never. He also always told me how jealous she was. After he retired, that was the first year he said he could not come to my house for Thanksgiving. He had to go to her sisters or she would be mad! He hated her cooking, and he always loved my kosher turkey. I knew he was not happy about it, but apparently, she had given him an ultimatum. He now had to spend holidays at her sister's house. It bothered me, but I never said much. If that was what he wanted to do, then so be it.

The summer months came again and his legs were worst now than ever. I had drove over to bring him some clothing and food. He had a blanket over his legs, so I could not see them. I pulled the blanket off his legs.

I yelled, "What the hell is the matter with you? You are going to die with your legs like this. They were literally blue! What is causing this?"

He did not know.

I said, "What about Linda? Doesn't she think you should be in a hospital? This is all fluid, and it is going to kill you."

I told him I knew a good doctor in Boston, and if he did not do something about it, it would kill him. I immediately went over to Linda's pharmacy. I was mad as hell. I walked in and saw her in the back. I was as nice as could be.

I said, "Have you seen the Doc's legs? Don't you think he needs medical attention?"

She blamed it all on him and said he did not want to go to a doctor. I said it has been almost two years now, and this is ridiculous as he cannot even walk. She acted all nice to me and said she would try to convince him to see a doctor.

I said, "If he doesn't, I am putting him in my car and driving him to Boston tomorrow!"

She said, "I'll take care of it. I'll take care of it."

I walked out so mad. I am thinking to myself, "This woman owns a pharmacy. There are four pharmacists here every day, and she does not know how to help the Doc? What the hell is going on here?" I started getting very very suspicious of her.

Three days later, he called me. He had been admitted to a local hospital. I ran to the hospital (which is not a very good one), and he was laying in the bed and his legs were almost normal. All the fluid was gone, and they had him on all kinds of meds. (After two years of not being able to get up or walk properly?) His legs looked 100 percent better, and he could walk much easier. After two years of swelling and pain? What the heck is going on here?

He assured me he was fine and eager to get back to his garden. I felt much better to see him in good spirits for once in two years. It was also nice to see him have normal legs.

In the back of my mind, I could not help thinking that Linda was poisoning his food. There was no explanation for the swelling in his legs. No doctor knew why. This pharmaceutical woman was now controlling his drug intake and life. She had access to any drug on the market! All she had to do is turn the key to her pharmacy!

I expressed my thoughts to Heather, my sisters, and anyone else I could tell. I said, "I swear she is poisoning him." Everyone thought he was too smart for that. Was he? After learning that her first husband died at forty-one of a massive heart attack in the pharmacy, my theory of this woman that I believed to have Munchausen syndrome was coming true!

After much research on Munchausen syndrome, it commonly occurs in mothers that kill their children or caretakers that kill their beloved mother, father, or boyfriend! Studies report that the majority of people with Munchausen syndrome by proxy are women who are often seen by friends and families and even medical personnel as extraordinarily loving companions who are vitally concerned about the health of their companion. People with Munchausen by proxy, before being arrested, have even won awards for their seemingly selfless devotion. This is exactly why they do what they do. They get attention, which only brings on more of their dangerous, destructive behavior. People with Munchausen syndrome make their patient sick and then rescue them and call for help.

Through the course of the next year, the Doc had fallen down in his home over three times, and guess who saved his life?

Apparently, she had continued to incapacitate him, and he had to stay at her house more often. When he requested to go home, she would drop him off; and within two hours, he had fallen down, fell asleep in the sun, and was burned. It was one thing after another. At that time, he had asked me to cut his grass. He was too ill, and no doctor could tell him what was wrong with him. At least, no local doctor. I would always say, "Why don't you go to Boston?" Linda did not want him anywhere but the same little local (terrible) hospital. He was getting regular blood transfusions now and still no one knew why! He had about two acres and a very big field. He knew I loved to do it, but I liked to cut the grass when he was there. She was not too happy about this new arrangement either. She would show up with her mad face and talk to him in a very demeaning manor. I had then realized that he had become dependent on her because he had to go to the same hospital all the time for blood transfusions and other testing. He did not have cancer, but still to this day, no one knows what caused his liver and kidney failure.

As I did my research on Munchausen syndrome, it confirmed to me that the person that has this illness often works in health care and knows a lot about medical care and medicine. She can describe the patient's symptoms in great medical detail. Also, she has the need to be very involved with the health care team and is liked by the staff for the care she gives her patient. *Bingo!* These women seem devoted to their patient, and it is very hard for health care professionals to see a diagnosis of Munchausen syndrome by proxy.

According to the US National Library of Medicine, the patient sees many health care providers and goes into the hospital a lot. They often have many tests or other procedures. The patient has strange symptoms that don't fit with any disease. The symptoms do not match the results. The patient's symptoms are reported by the caretaker. They are never seen by health care professionals. The symptoms go away in the hospital and then start again when the patient goes home. Most often, Munchausen syndrome by proxy goes undiagnosed.

My previous paragraph defines exactly the life the Doc was living. She was taking him back and forth to the same hospital for blood transfusions and other procedures and then would take him back to her house. This went on the last year of his life. I was more than suspicious, but it was hard for me to believe that she was killing him slowly. He had told me so many times how she had saved his life. I would get so angry and say, "What? She called an ambulance because an hour after she dropped you at your home, you fell down and were unconscious?" I would think, "What did she put in his food that morning?" She always told me how he liked her bacon and eggs! She also always told me that I did not know how much she did for him.

He told me to come to his house one day. He said that he had to move in with Linda due to his illnesses, but he was going to have her take him back to his house a few times a week. He hated being at her house. It was almost as if he wanted my approval. I asked him why he did not hire a nurse at his home and also told him that I would come and help him. He said that Linda would be too jealous. The Doc had nothing but money! He could have gone to the best hospitals and had the best home health care, but she would not allow it. She was going to take care of him! She was going to save him lots of money by taking him into her home!

He told me he hated being at her house because she stayed upstairs and did not go to bed until two o'clock in the morning. She did not get up until ten in the morning, and he was an early riser. A few days after I went to Linda's house to see him, a look of shock was on her face.

"What are you doing here?"

"I came to see the Doc."

I knew he could hear my voice, and he started calling to her.

"Linda, Linda, let her in."

I walked into a sunroom, and the Doc was shivering laying on a king-size air mattress. He told me he was freezing.

I said, "Of course you are. The air is what is cold, and you need a deflector on the mattress to keep the cold down."

She never did anything about the air bed. He complained he was freezing all the time. It was the air bed. He was laying there lifeless, and she was not very happy that I was there. I left there and called my sister that was a very avid camper. She knew everything there was about staying warm on an air mattress. She could not believe he was on a king-size air mattress with no deflector to keep the cold down. She could not believe he was on an air mattress and not in a bed! I was livid, but I could not do anything about it. I knew that my thoughts about her poisoning him were now true. He was being treated like a dog left to die!

CHAPTER 11

DNR

One Sunday morning about a week later, I went to her house at 11:30 a.m. She came to the door, and I could hear him yelling. She refused to let me in!

I said, "Linda, I want to see the Doc."

She said she had not gotten herself together yet and did not want any company. It was right then and there that I knew she was doing something very bad to my much loved doc. I called my sister, and I was outraged. I told her how she would not let me in the house at eleven thirty on a Sunday morning because *she* wasn't together yet? What about him? I could hear him yelling in the background, and I knew he always wanted to see me. This was bullshit. I knew that absolutely, positively, she was slowly killing him. The people of Eastport all thought she was the caring, loving woman that took such good care of him. She always told everyone, "You don't know how much I do for him." She repeatedly convinced people how she was his savior! Very common behavior for a woman with Munchausen syndrome and mental illness. She resented him and all the women that were still trying to call him. The previous time I was there, she came into the room viciously and took his cell phone away and said, "Who are you talking to now?" She did not want him talking to anyone, especially me. I played the devil's advocate just so I could have contact and told her what an angel she was to be taking care of him. I actually wanted to put my hands around her neck and choke her until she lost consciousness! I knew everything she said was *lies*! Why didn't she take him to a good doctor in Boston? He had the best medical insurance money could buy, and he had nothing but lots of money. Why was he laying on a king-size air mattress on the floor, freezing his ass off? He was supposedly so sick, and she was such a good caretaker. To this day, I have never heard a medical explanation about why his kidneys were failing. He ate healthier than any man I ever knew. He drank only tea and never smoked. I knew in my heart that she was hurting him, but he kept telling me that she was caring for him. He had no one else. All of his family lived in Egypt, and he did not have one relative in the United States. It was a simple plan for her. She knew that once he was really bad, her health proxy status would kick in; and then, she could do whatever she wanted with him. No one could say a word. At the time, I did not know that he had made her his health proxy. I also did not know that she had drove him to her lawyer's office and had him leave his entire estate including his home to her. We are talking about $4 million here folks! I would say she had a very big motive. Between the resentment she had toward him about other women, me, and never wanting to marry her, she justified what she was doing because she is a psychopath and she needed money very badly. Her little local pharmacy took a big hit during the past seven years. A Rite Aid pharmacy opened only four miles away. She still had to come up with a half a million a year to pay her four loyal pharmacists that had been there for forty-five years. The pharmacy to this day looks like it is going out of business—no stock on the shelves and no new products, only a functioning pharmacy that the old-timers in town still use. She needed money, and no one but me figured that out! He would have never believed it because she would have never told him. He would have never given her a nickel anyway for a failing business. We all know what happens to the little street corner pharmacy when a CVS or Rite Aid opens four miles away. They go out of business!

Unfortunately, all her workers and family never saw beyond her Mercedes and cheap clothes! I did! I knew she had a failing business, and I also knew that her plan was to kill the Doc and keep everything running just as smoothly as it is today. No one would suspect her because she was so nice. No one would think of her as a murderess, only me. I have very deep perceptions of people. I am able to see the telltale signs of someone deliberately hurting someone I love. She had been killing him slowly! I was the only one that knew! No one would have ever believed that she would be his murderous health proxy!

A few days passed, and I did not hear anything from him. I was getting very worried. I went to his house and it was dark and I could tell he had not been there. I went directly to Linda's house and continued to ring the doorbell. You could not see her Mercedes because it was in a closed garage. She also had just bought another. She had bought herself a new Mercedes utility vehicle to match her convertible. He was sick and dying, and she was shopping for new cars? This bothered me a great deal. My suspicions were extremely high.

At that time, I did not know that she was his health proxy, and I did not know that she and her lawyer controlled his entire estate. I had thought that he had made a will many years ago. I also believed that Heather that had worked for him for thirty years would be a beneficiary in his will.

I stood at Linda's house holding the doorbell. I wanted to see him or know where he was. No answer. As I walked to my car, her sister was driving in the driveway. She was an older woman and uneducated and did as Linda said. I asked her where the Doc was. She said he was in the local hospital. I jumped in my car and drove there immediately. Apparently, he had been there a few days, but Linda never called or told anyone. After all, his family lived in Egypt. Apparently, she thought there was no one to tell. She certainly did not want me around because she knew I was more than suspicious at this point.

I got to the hospital, and he had been operated on. The doctors had put a port in the top part of his left arm so he could have dialysis.

She was not there, thank God. I was so happy to see him, and he was so happy to see me. I sat on the bed and asked him how he was feeling. He was the most coherent I had seen in a year. His eyes were alert, and he was even joking with me. I had gone to the Lebanese market and brought him some fresh tabouli and candies. He was eating like a horse. I was feeding him when Linda walked into the room. I could see the contempt on her face. I acted normal and said how great he was doing. She sat in the chair on the side of his bed like a Nazi guard. Then, she asked me if I had seen her new Mercedes. I am thinking to myself, "Lady, you have got to be kidding me." I wanted to kill her with my bare hands! He is laying here trying to recuperate from his operation, and she wants me to look out the window at her second Mercedes? Oh God, I hated this woman now! Forgive me!

I told him I would see him soon and left. I could see right through her now, and I knew she was not helping him; she was hurting him.

That night, I went to the hospital just before visiting hours were over so I did not run into her again. He was so happy I was there. I rubbed my hand through his hair and asked him how he was. He said he was in a lot of pain, but he was getting better. His arms were dry, so I started rubbing some moisturizer on them. I looked down at his wrist and saw a big purple bracelet that said *DNR*! I completely lost it! I asked him, "Why do you have this on your arm? The doctors told me you were going to be okay. You just need dialysis." He said Linda told him it was to *help* him! Now, I knew that everything I thought to be true was true! I told him that DNR meant do not resuscitate! I explained to him that even if he was home and fell down and could not breathe, they would not give him oxygen! I called the nurse in and had her explain what DNR was. He truly did not know what it meant! Linda told him that it was to help him! I could see a sudden change come over him. He started picking at the bracelet.

"Take it off," he shouted at me.

I took my car key and ripped it off! I said, "Why the hell does she have this on you? Are you sure you trust this woman?"

The nurse explained to him that he would have to talk to the doctor in the morning and only he could have it taken off his chart. The next morning came, and that is exactly what he did.

That day, I made sure that Heather went to see him to cheer him up. I also met Dr. Gardner there. They had been friends for forty years. He proceeded to tell Dr. Gardner the stories about when we went to Italy and all the money I spent. We laughed and laughed!

He was becoming his old self again. Heather and I had both told him that when he gets out of the hospital, he could go home and we would go there to help him. That made him very happy. After Heather left, he expressed to me that Linda would be very jealous of Heather and I and would not like it. I got very tough with him and told him that I did not think she was doing right by him. I questioned the DNR, and I know he was thinking about it. I now knew he knew she had deceived him. We talked about good times. I said to him, "You always complained about the money I spent, but you know I have had a good life." Then, I asked him, "Are you dying?"

He said, "Absolutely not."

The doctors had told him that all he needed was rehab to get his strength back. I told him he could come to my house and I would get him better. He smiled and said Linda would never allow it and he did not want to hurt her. He said she had saved his life so many times.

I downplayed his excuses and said, "Please, what did she do? Call an ambulance?" I told him to stop telling me how much she has done for him because I hear it enough from her.

It was the next night after I had removed the DNR bracelet from his arm. I went there late in the evenings to avoid her. She was walking down the hall, coming toward me with a very mean face on.

She said, "Who do you think you are?"

I said, "What the hell are you talking about?"

She said, "Who are you to have him taking bracelets off his arm?"

I said, "Why does he need a DNR?"

She was livid. She said, "You do not know how sick he is."

I said, "No, I don't. Why don't you tell me?"

She said I had better not mention a word of what she said to me to the Doc and the DNR had better be back on his arm when she returned tomorrow or there would be hell to pay!

I said, "What the hell is wrong with you? Don't ever tell me what to do. He does not need a DNR on his arm when he is trying to recuperate."

She was out of her mind. How dare I? Well, I dared. Now, I knew she wanted him dead!

During this time, the only thing I said to him was what he had always said to me. I told him, "Remember what you said to me when I became successful?"

He said, "What?"

"You told me that *never* tell the person that you are leaving your money to that they are the one getting it." I watched his face, and I knew he was now thinking that my suspicions were very warranted.

After she accosted me in the hallway, I went straight to his room and said, "That woman is a psychopath, and you had better be careful. Are you sure you trust her because I sure don't?"

He said nothing. I knew he was thinking about all the events that had transpired and especially about the DNR she had placed on his arm. She had made him feel so indebted to her because she had him thoroughly convinced that she had saved his life so many times. This was such bullshit! She probably drugged him before she used to drop him off at his house so he would fall and die! I would always bring him the Egyptian food he loved, and that really pissed her off. The day before he was going to be moved to the rehab of her choice, she came walking into the room and said, "I got you a lobster roll from McDonald's."

"Oh dear God," I thought to myself! I wonder what it is laced with. He assured me that she would call or text me that night to let me know what rehab facility she was putting him in, and he wanted me there the next day.

CHAPTER 12

The Death Call

That Friday night after I left the hospital, I received a short text from Linda stating that he had been moved to Harper Home. This rehab facility was just four miles from the hospital he was in. Linda wanted him to be somewhere that would be convenient for her, on and off the highway.

Saturday morning around eight, I drove over there as quickly as possible. The place looked nice from the outside, but when I walked inside, I felt nauseous. All I could smell was feces and urine! It permeated the air. I could not believe that this is where she had put him. There were people lying on beds in the hallways that looked like they were dead. Other patients were roaming the halls unattended. What a dump! I went to the desk and asked for his room number. I ran down the hallway as his room was almost at the very end. He was laying there in his own feces and told me he had been pushing the button for two hours. I ran down to the desk and said I needed someone immediately to clean him up and help. They asked me who I was. I stated my name and the girl said to me, "You are not Linda?"

I said, "No, I am not, but he has been asking for help for two hours and no one has helped him."

She was rude and miserable. It was apparent to me at that time that they all knew who they had to answer to and it certainly was not me. Apparently, Linda's niece worked in the administration in these types of places while she was getting her pharmacist license. She had got him the bed in this horrible, depressing home. It was a nightmare. He was so depressed. Just a day before, he was so happy in the hospital and so upbeat. Now, he looked like he was dying.

"I have to get out of here," he said to me.

"I am going to get you out of here, and I do not give a shit what Linda has to say about it. You had better tell her that I am finding you a new place as soon as possible. I am going home and getting on the computer and finding the best facility that money can buy. All you have is money. You need rehab and care right now, and this is a horrible place."

He totally agreed with me, and he was so sad and beside himself.

"How the hell could she put you in this dump?" I asked.

He knew I loved him and cared about him. This was not about money. This was about life or death. Johnny NY went there to see him, and his reaction to me was, "She is trying to kill him. I would have wanted to die if someone had put me in that hell hole! No doctors, no RNs, only CNAs or nurse assistants. It was unreal! The rooms were so dark and dreary. They still had the old television mounts on the walls. This place was a decaying death hole. He could afford to go anywhere."

I held his hand tightly and said, "You better talk to her, and you better tell her that we are moving you out of here as soon as possible."

He said, "Okay."

I also asked him when his first dialysis treatment was because I knew he had to have it.

He said, "Monday."

I sat there and wanted to start crying because I could not believe this horrible depressing place he was in. I had brought him a nice bath robe and something to snack on, but he did not want anything. The food they gave him was not even edible. I waited until they finally came and cleaned him up and stayed holding his hand. He had told me that she was coming there around eleven when she got out of bed. He knew I was fit to be tied. He knew I was pissed and ready for a fight, and he knew I did not trust her and I did not feel she had his best interest at heart. The situation was bad enough, so I tried to control my anger. I rubbed his hair back, but I could see him getting weaker by the minute.

"Are you going to be okay?"

Linda is coming this afternoon," he said.

I said, "Somehow, that does not comfort me at all. I have got to get you out of here."

He knew me very well, and he knew I would verbally fight with her. I sensed that he wanted me to go before she came. The week that had passed, he had left several messages on my phone asking me when I was going to come to see him. That was when he was in the hospital. I was there twice a day. Once in the early morning and then late at night after she left. I still have a Gandhi book that he gave to me in the hospital that one of his ex-lovers had given to him while he was in the hospital. He did not want Linda to see it, so he gave it to me. Apparently, she was jealous of everyone.

After eighteen years, Linda was now an obese, gray haired, unattractive, miserable old woman with badly nicotine-stained teeth. I told him I loved him as I did every time I left, and I said I would see him in the morning, which would be Sunday. He knew I went to a little chapel for mass near my house every Sunday and knew it would not be until after ten that I would come the next day.

As I was leaving the parking lot, Linda pulled on the side of me with her new Mercedes and said, "Nice place, isn't it?"

I looked at her and said vehemently, "I wouldn't let one of my dogs stay here."

She was not happy with me. I drove away. "Fuck her," I thought to myself.

I ran home to my computer and called everywhere that was a five-star facility. I located a place that was not far away that had top ratings and overlooked the ocean. I knew this would be perfect for him. It was expensive, but that was not an issue. She had him in a welfare facility because his insurance paid every nickel. I printed out all the information and had an appointment with the woman I had spoken to on the phone. Now, all I had to do is to show him the papers and get him to agree to tell Linda that this is where he will be going on Wednesday. The facility had a room for him and was ready to take him the next day.

Sunday came and I went to the chapel. I was crying my eyes out, and the pastor asked me what was wrong. I asked if the whole chapel could pray for the Doc as he needs our prayers. It was quite obvious to everyone there that I was beside myself. We prayed.

I left the chapel and looked at my cell phone that I had left in the car. I saw that he had called me. I tried to call him back, but there was no answer. I went home and took the only Lladro figurine I had left—a girl with three dalmatians. I knew how he loved looking at the Lladros, and I could not go into his house anymore. Linda put a stop to that. I was still cutting his grass every week, all two acres, but I enjoyed doing it. I loved to tell him that the place looked great.

I ran into the rehab facility with the Lladro in hand and some pastry. Once again, he was wet in the bed. I was on fire! I ran down to the desk and asked why is he laying in his own urine. They snapped back at me and told me I was not Linda and they only had to listen to his health proxy! It became apparent at that moment that she was waiting to let his health continue to fail so her health proxy status was in full force.

I walked back in the room with the paperwork from the beautiful place I wanted him to go. I told him it was all arranged and I placed the Lladro on a little table near him. A big smile came across his face the minute he saw the Lladro, the little girl with the three dalmatians. I told him that at least he would have something to look at that was pretty. I also brought a nice blanket from my home to put on his bed. I had noticed that he did not eat any breakfast as the tray was there and had not been touched. He was already very thin and needed all the nutrition he could get. He had no appetite. He was very weak and seemed to be getting weaker as I sat there. Within an hour, I could see him failing even more. I told him that he had to go for dialysis tomorrow because he was getting too weak. He then informed me that Linda had canceled his dialysis treatment because he was not strong enough. "No shit." He wasn't strong enough because it had been almost a week and he had not had the dialysis. He needed dialysis to function. I knew she was coming and I had to get out of there. I told him that he had better tell her that he was going to the new place that I have made arrangements for. He was very weak and said, "Okay."

I drove home crying my eyes out! I knew I had to contact Dr. Gardner, our longtime friend. I needed him to come to this rehab home to see the condition the Doc was in. Dr. Gardner lived across the street from me and was a wonderful, honest, and brilliant man. He was very well respected throughout many nearby towns including Eastport. He had a fabulous reputation as being a great doctor. I called him crying, and he said, "What is wrong?"

I said, "Please come with me this afternoon to see the Doc? He needs to be back in the hospital. He is failing by the hour."

In his warm and kind way, he said he would come right over and pick me up and we would go right away.

Dr. Gardner had never met Linda. I had described her, and I also told him my thoughts on her lack of care for the Doc. He knew how I loved the Doc and listened to every word I said. He had never seen me that upset before.

We arrived at the Harper rehab, and Dr. Gardner's first impression was very similar to mine.

"What is he doing in a place like this?" he asked.

"I have no idea. Linda thinks this place is wonderful."

He was not impressed. We got to the door of his room, and Linda had her head back sleeping in the chair on the side of the Doc's bed. The Doc was having tremors! Dr. Gardner immediately went in and called him by name.

"Sahib."

The Doc grabbed Dr. Gardner's arm and called out his first name, "Hi Henry." And then, he fell back into delirium.

Dr. Gardner was outraged as he looked at the Doc's dried up lips and dehydrated mouth. Linda woke and said to Dr. Gardner, "Who are you?"

He said, "I am a lifetime friend of Sahib and a doctor."

Dr. Gardner then asked why there were no glycerin sticks near his bed for his mouth. He got up quickly and ran down to the front desk. Linda looked at me with hatred in her eyes, and I glared right back at her. Dr. Gardner came back and ran the glycerin sticks over the Doc's lips. Linda then lashed out at me and said, "Did you take the bracelet off of him?"

"What bracelet?" I replied.

She said, "Well, you seem to be good at taking bracelets off of him."

I looked at her and said, "I did not take anything off his arm, and don't do this right now."

I could see that Dr. Gardner was now believing everything I had told him about this cantankerous witch! He explained to Linda that the Doc did not look well and needed medical care. Her response was, "He does this all the time." The Doc was literally thrashing in the bed and incoherent. He would come in and out and say a few words, but it was obvious that he was slipping into delirium from not having any dialysis. Dr. Gardner suggested to her that he should immediately be back in the hospital and his symptoms were not normal. She could have cared less, and no one was going to tell her what he needed. She informed Dr. Gardner that she had been taking care of him for the past year and he always did this. I had to get out of there! Dr. Gardner told me he had never seen such an idiot in his life. He could not believe the callousness of the rehab facility. Dr. Gardner was now very upset watching his longtime friend suffering at the hands of his health proxy.

Monday morning, I went back at eight and they had him up and slumped over in a chair. He was sitting alone and looked like he was dead. He grabbed my hand and begged me to get him out of there.

He said, "I told Steve (his friend that had visited him there) that I wanted him to get my lawyer here to change my will."

Steve then called Linda! The lawyer was supposed to come on Thursday. Linda had set the appointment! This was the death call! I ran to my car and called Linda. I was crying my eyes out. I said, "Please, please, get him back to the hospital."

She snapped at me and said, "Don't tell me what to do."

Again, I called Dr. Gardner. I could not go back and see him that way. I ran to his lawyer's office and left him a letter begging him to please go to the rehab facility to see his physical state. The lawyer was not there. Dr. Gardner had assured me that he was driving over there and making sure that he was brought to a hospital. About an hour later, I called the lawyer's office (her lawyer), and I begged him to go to the rehab. He laughed and told me not to get so upset that Linda is taking good care of him!

I said, "No, she isn't. He is suffering and thrashing in the bed. He needs medical attention, and he is in a hell hole over there."

The lawyer, a local blowhard, could have cared less.

Dr. Gardner went there and called me. He said, "I told her she had better get him into a hospital." He then went to the local police department to file an elder abuse report on her. The Eastport police would not take his report. We later found out that her niece, a pharmacist in her pharmacy and his second health proxy, was married to a local police officer. When Dr. Gardner told me that, I sent her a text message and told her that if he was not taken to a hospital, I was going to the state police and filing a report against her. Thirty minutes after my text, Dr. Gardner called me and informed me that Linda had just called him and said that doc was going back to the hospital. I was so relieved. I thought now I could actually save him from this murderous woman.

I waited about an hour and called the hospital. They told me he was in the emergency room and to call back in about an hour and they would tell me what room he was in.

I called back in an hour, and they said they had never heard of him and have no medical records on him. It was as if he did not exist anymore.

I said, "What the hell are you talking about? They just told me an hour ago that he was in the emergency room."

She said, "We have no record of that patient."

I explained to her that he had been there for two weeks some four days ago. She still had no patient with his name.

I called Dr. Gardner, and he had said that his ex-wife had also gone over to the rehab and they would not give her any information as to his whereabouts either.

I sent a text to Linda. "Where is the Doc?" No reply. I continued texting her, and she never responded. This went on for the next three days. By that time, I had stated to her in the texts that I knew exactly what she was doing. She was killing the Doc. The next day, the Eastport police were waiting at my gate. I knew the officer.

He said, "I am sorry but Linda has put a protective order against you, and you are not to go near her house or her business." He made me sign the document, and I was given a date to show up in court two weeks later. Why couldn't anyone know where he was? Why couldn't anyone see him? Why did she put a protective order against me? I was going to all the local hospitals and back to the hospital he was in. The nurses that took care of him there wanted to help me, and they informed me that she must have put a "No Information" order on him. Only the health proxy can do this. She was killing him slowly and not giving him the medical care he needed. I called every-one that he was close to. I called Heather and asked her to call Linda. I knew Linda would respond to Heather as she worked right next door to her pharmacy since the animal hospital had closed. Heather called me later that evening and said that Linda said he was very sick and she did not want anyone bothering him. I told Heather that she was letting him die. Dr. Gardner went to Heather's workplace the next day and explained to her that he had tried to file an elder abuse report on Linda because of the physical state of suffering the Doc was in. Heather now believed that everything I had been telling her was now coming true. Heather also thought that Linda had her own money and would not do such a horrendous thing, but she still could not understand why no one could know where he was and no one was allowed to see him.

Many people and local veterinarians kept calling me to ask me where he was. They called Linda to try to get information, but no one was allowed to know where he was or to see him. Two weeks later, I was on my way home from his house after cutting his grass. The previous veterinarian that I had worked for, who gave me my recommendation when I went to work for Doc, called me. I looked down at my phone and answered with hopes that he had some information.

He said, "Doc is dead!"

I hung up the phone and started screaming, crying to the top of my lungs in the car! I was not able to save him from this murderous bitch!

When I was cutting his lawn the day he died, a feeling had come over me, and it was almost as if I could feel him calling out my name.

I still sit here and wonder why I was incapable of saving him from this murderous health proxy? She inherited his entire estate, over four million, plus his house that contained all of my beautiful collections. The blow hard lawyer, who would not go to see him when I begged, did not notify his family in Egypt until over one month after his death. None of them came to the states because he had left them some properties and a good sum of money. They were told that he left everything here to his longtime companion.

There were no services, no graveside prayers. Heather's plot is on the side of his and worked for him thirty years and was not allowed to attend his burial.

I stood in the parking lot of a local restaurant across the street from the cemetery. She pulled up in her new Mercedes and stood there while the coffin was lowered into the ground. As soon as she left, I ran over to his grave and laid on top of it crying and telling him how sorry I was that I could not save him.

I write this story so my reader can decide for themselves what the truth of these circumstances that surround his death conclude.

I am a very spiritual person; and after the loss of my mom, dad, and the Doc, I believe that no one ever dies inside of you if you keep them alive. The day he died and I was cutting his grass, I noticed that his favorite tree, a mimosa tree, had a small baby growing from its root. I knelt down and cleared the grass from around it and mulched it and watered it. I moved away from the small coastal town of Eastport. I now live in the South. A nearby friend invited me to her house, and the yard was full of beautiful mimosa trees. I saw hundreds of seed pods on the ground and asked if I could have a few. She let me take as many as I wanted. I planted about ten small pots in my greenhouse, and the trees grew. They are about three feet tall now.

Every day, I sit outside at a table near my back door to drink my tea. Apparently, I had left the remainder of the mimosa seeds on that table. I now have twenty seven-foot tall mimosa trees that I did *not* plant on the side of my table. He is still with me every day and given me the amazing ability to transform my pain into love through my writing. No one ever dies unless you let them. Their spirit is always with you and is better than any friend.

He died on a Wednesday. He was buried on Saturday morning. It took three days for him to be buried? The same amount of time it takes to send a body for cremation and have the ashes back in hand.

Unfortunately, the two weeks before his death, in my text messages that I was prevented from sending any further (due to the protective order she had placed on herself against me), I had stated that she had better not cremate him because it was against his Muslim religion. I knew he had bought the plot in the cemetery some forty years beforehand. In the Muslim religion, just like Jews, the deceased is buried the very next day. Why did it take three days?

I would bet the farm that there is a small cardboard box of ashes in that very expensive coffin that was placed in the ground. What do you think?

A Special Thanks

The message in my book of transforming pain into love through my writing also came from a great loss that I experienced during a time when this book was in its infancy. An extraordinary, loving, caring lady, Lynda Byrd.

I was power washing Lynda's house on a very hot day here in the South. During my lunch breaks, I would tell Lynda of my sadness about the ill fate of the much loved veterinarian that is the main character of this book. Lynda spent her life teaching at a very prestigious school as an English teacher. She listened to my story wholeheartedly. She had the most wonderful expressions, and her special brand of magic would have encouraged anyone to pursue their thoughts of writing a book. Lynda was an animal lover just like me. Her dog Brody was always at her side.

We had so many similarities due to losses we had both suffered in our lives concerning the deaths of people we loved deeply. Lynda gave me the ability to focus on what is invincible, *love* because it can never be destroyed. Through her wisdom, I was able to reinvent my pain into love through my writing.

She watched me work tirelessly and many times begged me to stop working because she did not want me to overwork, or exert myself in the heat. Lynda was a "real" person which is a very rare commodity these days. I was not just the "power washing lady" to Lynda, I was someone special.

I am sure that Lynda made everyone feel that way due to her actions as I worked at her home. She would bring out packages of wafer cookies, water, and soda, and always tell me to take a break. Her caring for me in the little time that we had together made me realize that once in a lifetime, you do meet someone that understands you and listens, but most of all, truly cares about you. Actions do speak louder than words but with Lynda, it was a combination that was intertwined that will live within my soul forever.

After working at her home for a few days, my job was finished. She insisted that I did not charge her enough money and presented me with a beautiful gift.

As I unwrapped the package, it contained a beautiful blank journal with the word "Life" written across the front of it. In small letters, the cover read, "We are each a part of all that surrounds us. Embrace the miracle of life."

Less than a year later, Lynda passed away suddenly. I was beside myself and cried uncontrollably when I read it in the local town newspaper. I could not believe what I had just read! We were close in age, and it affected me more so that I did not know of her passing, and I did not attend her services.

I immediately ran to the journal she had given to me and read her inscription once again.

Dawn,

This is for your notes, ♡ for your book I can hardly wait to read ♡.

Luv U,
Lynda Byrd

I have truly enjoyed getting to know you ♡.

Her symbolism and her words said it all . . . she believed in me, and she made sure I knew it.

Transforming pain into love is one of the most difficult tasks we all face when someone we care about and love dies. I am a firm believer that we are put on this earth to keep their love and their light glowing.

Lynda is my light, and I will continue to shine because of the gift that she continues to give me every day. On my darkest days, I reach for my journal and read Lynda's inscription. Then dark turns into light!

About the Author

Dawn Liss is an avid animal lover and also a seven-time marathon runner. Her list of accomplishments is impressive: degrees in political science, law, surgical technician for animals, a stint as a professional singer, and years of experience in retail management as a successful entrepreneur. She published her own "free" animal magazine in the early 2000s, "The Furry Friends Frolics." Dawn was featured in *Woman's World* magazine in their October 14, 2003, edition as an "Animal Angel." She has spent her entire life dedicated to taking care of animals. She generated money for her Furry Friends Fund some seventeen years ago. The fund was set up to help pay the vet costs for people who could not afford much needed medical care for their animals, especially the elderly. She has been called a hurricane, but those that know the vivacious and talented blond businesswoman prefer to think of her as a gentle storm.

Very Truly Yours,

Dawn

Printed in the USA
CPSIA information can be obtained
at www.ICGtesting.com
JSHW071713131223
53712JS00012B/133